Sonrise Stable
Rosie and Scamper

Vicki Watson

Illustrated by
Janet Griffin-Scott

Printed in the United States of America

ISBN 978-0-9847242-0-8

Library of Congress Control Number: 2017900732

Second edition: 2017

The questions in the back of the book may be discussed after reading each chapter.

Sonrise Stable Characters
(Horses in Parentheses)

Grandma *(Kezzie)*

Kristy and Eric Jackson
- Rosie *(Jet)*

Lisa and Robert
- Lauren

Julie *(Elektra)* and Jonathan
- Jared *(Scout)*
- Jessie *(Patches)*
- Jamie *(Pearl)*

Carrie Rogers
Judy and Ross Robinson, Carrie's foster parents
Barn cats: Katy and Jemimah

Sonrise Stable Map

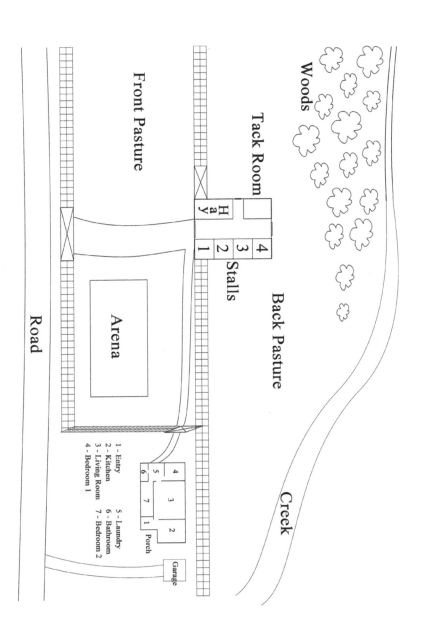

Woods

Front Pasture

Tack Room

Stalls

H a y

4 3 2 1

Back Pasture

Arena

Road

Creek

4 3 2 1 Porch

6 5 7

Garage

1 - Entry
2 - Kitchen
3 - Living Room
4 - Bedroom 1

5 - Laundry
6 - Bathroom
7 - Bedroom 2

1
Rosie and Jet

"There's Grandma's house!" Rosie's mother was the only other person in the car, so there was no need for this announcement. Certainly Kristy knew they were approaching the very house she had grown up in, but Rosie couldn't resist. She'd begun announcing their arrival at her grandmother's house when she was just a toddler, and it made her smile every time she did it.

The car slowed as they passed the barn entrance and the Sonrise Stable sign with its horse and cross. Kristy turned in to the second drive at the house. Rosie waited anxiously for the car to stop, then she pulled the door latch and jumped out. The small, wiry nine-year-old ran toward the porch of the one-and-a-half story farmhouse nestled in the trees, her dark, braided pigtails bouncing wildly.

"Whoa, girl! How about some help here?"

Rosie skidded to a stop and doubled back toward her mother.

"Take this." Kristy tossed a sleeping bag her way.

Rosie reached for the dark-blue bag, catching it more with her face than her hands. "Oomph! Sorry, Mom. I just can't wait to see Grandma—and Jet." She tucked the sleeping bag under one arm and grabbed her helmet from the back seat.

Grandma stepped through the front door onto the porch. Working with horses over the years had kept her trim, and she was still strong enough to toss bales of hay around.

Kristy wrestled with a suitcase that was stuck between the seats. She gave a jerk, and it popped free.

"I thought Rosie was spending a few days. I didn't realize she was moving in," Grandma joked.

"It *is* only for a few days. We'd need a moving van to bring all her things out here." Kristy grabbed a backpack and pillow with her other hand and started toward the porch.

There was no denying the three were related. They shared the same slim build, dark-brown hair and eyes, and quick, easy smile.

Rosie dropped the sleeping bag on the porch by the front door. "I'm ready to ride!" She pulled a bag of carrots out of her helmet and grinned. "For Jet."

"You've spoiled that pony. Whenever I go to the barn, she looks right past me to see whether you're coming too."

"I'm not spoiling her," Rosie laughed. "Carrots are healthy treats."

Grandma knelt down. "I've been looking forward to this weekend. Do I get a hug?"

Rosie wrapped her arms around her grandmother's neck. There wasn't anyone she loved more—except her mom and dad, of course. She'd grown even closer to her grandmother as they had worked together with the horses that summer.

Kristy set the rest of Rosie's things down next to the sleeping bag. "I sure miss living in the country. I can't wait until we can afford to move out of our subdivision."

"You're welcome to visit anytime," Grandma said. "You'll be able to move someday. God's timing is not always the same as ours."

"I know," Kristy sighed. "I try to be patient."

Grandma nodded. "I'm still learning patience myself after fifty-some years."

Fifty years? Rosie couldn't imagine what it would be like to be that old. And patience? She barely had any of that at all. Like right now. She wished they could go straight to the barn so she could ride Jet.

Kristy glanced at her watch. "Oh, dear! Is it that late already? Eric will be wondering what happened to me." She held out her arms to Rosie. "Hey girlie, give me a goodbye kiss. You help Grandma—and take good care of that pony. Love you." Kristy waved as she hurried back to her car.

"I love you too. Bye, Mom."

"Enjoy your time together," Grandma called out. She waved and then turned to her granddaughter. "I know we will, right?"

Rosie smiled and nodded. Spending four days with her grandmother and the horses was more exciting to her than a trip to Disney World.

Grandma put her hand on Rosie's shoulder. "Let's get this stuff inside. When you're settled, we'll go to the barn. Do you want to stay in your mom's room?"

"Why do you always call it Mom's room?" Rosie grabbed the suitcase, which weighed nearly as much as she did. "It's been a long time since Mom lived here."

"I don't know. I just never did anything else with those rooms after my girls moved out." Grandma picked up the other items, and they went inside.

When Rosie reached the staircase, she set her suitcase down and pulled it, thumping up one step at a time. At the halfway point, she looked back and noticed her grandmother smiling at her.

"Need a hand?"

"No." She gave a big tug and advanced another step.

Rosie had been born prematurely with a heart condition, and had spent the first few months of her life in the hospital. Because of her health issues and the fact that she was their only child, Kristy and Eric were especially cautious with her. Rosie was still small for her age, but she had grown much stronger over the past year.

Although she had ridden Jet before, someone had always been leading the pony. That summer her parents had finally agreed to let her begin riding Jet on her own. Grandma had taught many children to ride, and Rosie became her next eager student.

After tossing her clothes in the bedroom dresser, Rosie walked to the shelves on the opposite wall that held the awards her mother and aunts, Julie and Lisa, had won when they were younger.

She traced her finger over the gold horse that stood proudly atop one of the trophies. *Someday Jet and I will win trophies just like this.* She picked up a silky blue ribbon and turned it over. "First Place, Trail Class—Kristy & Ebony," her grandmother had written on it years ago.

Rosie was consumed with horses. She read, dreamed, and talked constantly about them. Her mom called it "horse

4

fever" and said it was hereditary. Kristy had inherited it from Grandma and then passed it on to Rosie.

Sometimes, instead of doing her schoolwork, she daydreamed about horses and sketched them in her notebook. Grandma said there was no cure for it. That was fine with Rosie. This was one illness she didn't want to recover from.

Rosie smiled, set the ribbon down, and reached for a small, framed photograph of her mother riding Ebony. *Mom sure looks a lot like me—or I look a lot like her. And Jet looks like Ebony. Jet—oh! I need to get over to the barn!* Rosie placed the picture back on the shelf and raced out of the room.

Grandma looked up as she clattered down the stairs. "Are you finally ready to ride? I thought you were taking a nap up there."

"Oh, Grandma." She was used to her grandmother's kidding and could, almost always, tell when she was being teased. "Where are my boots?"

"In the laundry room, right where you left them last time."

Rosie ran to retrieve her riding boots. She tripped trying to insert her foot into one of the boots as she walked back to the living room.

"Slow down there, girl," Grandma laughed. "We have all weekend. Bring a few of your carrots, and put the rest of the bag in the refrigerator."

Grandma held the back door open, and the two stepped onto the gravel path that led to the barn. Bordering the path on the right was a ravine that dropped down to a winding, bubbling creek. A grassy pasture stretched from their left to the road. Today, however, Rosie was blind to the natural beauty surrounding her. Four straight days of riding were in store, and she couldn't wait to get started.

"What have I been teaching you?"

Rosie pranced around her grandmother. "Keep my reins even, not too tight and not too loose, don't jerk on her mouth, stay balanced, and—oh, Grandma, you've told me so much. I don't see how I can remember it all!"

"You've remembered the most important things, but *knowing* and *doing* aren't always the same. You'll be a real rider when you do all those things without even thinking about them."

Rosie wanted to be a *real* rider, and maybe even a horse trainer someday, like her Aunt Julie. She looked ahead at the faded, white barn. Four stalls faced the house, each with two doors. One of the stall doors opened into the pasture and the other into the barn aisle. When the weather was nice, Grandma liked the horses to be outside as much as possible.

A jet-black pony poked her head over the first door and watched as they approached. Rosie took off running, and Jet hurried to the inside door of her stall where she greeted Rosie with a friendly nicker. Anticipating a treat, a pair of big brown eyes followed the girl's every move.

Rosie brushed the pony's thick forelock to the side, revealing a white star. "Jet, you're the most beautiful pony in the world." She put her hands on each side of the pony's head and kissed her velvety muzzle. Jet broke free from her grasp and tossed her head as if nodding in agreement.

Rosie pulled the biggest carrot out of her pocket and snapped it in two. She carefully flattened her hand, as her grandmother had taught her, and held out one of the pieces. Jet's soft lips brushed her palm as she took the carrot. Rosie felt a light, tingly sensation pass down her arm. "Ooh, Jet! That tickles."

Grandma unlatched the stall door and led the pony into the aisle. She rubbed Jet's neck affectionately. "She's so much like her mother. Ebony was one of my best ponies. She taught your mom to ride, as Jet is teaching you. After my three girls outgrew Ebony, many of my riding students took lessons on her."

"I'll never outgrow Jet! I'm going to ride her until I'm really old—like you."

"Hmm. Just how old do you think I am?" Grandma shook her head. "Oh, never mind. I don't even want to know. Come on. Let's get this pony brushed and saddled."

The two worked together quietly. Rosie was so absorbed in grooming Jet, it was a while before she noticed that her grandmother was no longer helping. Grandma leaned against the stall door, smiling.

Rosie paused. "What are you smiling about?"

"For a moment there, I thought I had gone back in time twenty years, and I was watching your mom and Ebony."

Grandma picked up a comb and began to work on a tangle in Jet's mane.

Rosie brushed the pony's soft black hair vigorously in circles with a rubber currycomb, then stopped to run her fingers through Jet's coat. "She's getting all fluffy."

"Yes, she's beginning to get her winter coat."

"But it's not even cold yet."

"Horses can't wait until the first snowfall to put on a coat, like you can," Grandma explained. "They start growing their winter coat early, so when it does get cold, they're ready."

"How do they know to do that?" Rosie asked.

"That's one of the mysteries of God's creation. It's triggered somehow by the number of daylight hours. When the days grow shorter, their coats grow longer."

Rosie hit a particularly itchy spot, and Jet raised her head, stretching her neck out in a funny position. She brushed harder, and Jet extended her neck more. "I know you love me scratching your itchy spot, but you're wearing my arm out." She groaned and leaned against the pony's shoulder for a short break.

Rosie tossed the currycomb into the tack bucket and pawed around until she found a hoof pick. Standing at Jet's left side, she ran her hand slowly down the pony's front leg and lifted her foot. Rosie held the hoof up and picked it clean, then carefully set it down, repeating the process for each hoof until she was back where she started.

Grandma laid a red wool blanket on the pony's back, slid it into place, and smoothed out the wrinkles. She set a black western saddle on top of the blanket. "You're growing so fast, it won't be long before you're tall enough to saddle Jet yourself. Do you remember how to tighten the girth?"

"Of course, Grandma. A real cowgirl has to saddle her own horse, you know." Rosie fed the leather strap through the ring in the girth and looped it up through the ring in the saddle. She pulled slowly and gradually until the girth was snug.

"You're getting good at that! Did I ever tell you about the time I didn't tighten the girth enough on my pony, Dolly?"

Rosie had heard the story before—so many times in fact that she'd stopped counting, but before she could say anything, her grandmother continued.

"As I cantered across the field, the saddle tipped more and more." Grandma leaned over to demonstrate. "Finally, I was so far sideways, I fell off. I wasn't hurt, just a bit frightened. But I learned my lesson! I never forgot to check the girth after that."

Rosie put her helmet on and fastened the buckle. "I can't imagine you as a little girl."

"Oh yeah? What do you think—I was always this old? I used to be a scrawny little horse-crazy girl just like you."

Rosie stood as straight and tall as she could. She knew her grandmother didn't mean anything by it, but she was tired of being smaller than other kids her age. "I'm not scrawny!"

"I know." Grandma squeezed her shoulder. "You're growing like a weed." She held the headstall of the bridle in her right hand and guided the snaffle bit into the pony's mouth with her left. Grandma gently tucked Jet's ears under the bridle, then pointed to the throatlatch.

Rosie fastened the buckle of the leather strap, and kissed Jet's muzzle. "I have the best pony in the world!" She turned and hugged her grandmother's waist. "And the best grandmother!"

2

Rosie's Surprise

Y ou're my favorite Rosie in the world!" Grandma
handed Jet's reins to her granddaughter, and they
walked side by side to the arena.

"Need any help getting—" Before Grandma could finish
her question, Rosie had her foot in the stirrup and, with a little
spring, was on the pony's back. Grandma laughed. "You'll be
giving *me* riding lessons before long!"

Rosie beamed. Everyone in her family rode horses—her
grandmother, parents, aunts, uncles, and cousins. Rosie
couldn't wait until she could ride as well as everyone else. Well,
she and her dad were about equal. Eric didn't have much time
to ride, but he had occasionally ridden Kezzie alongside Rosie
and Jet that summer, with Grandma giving him a few pointers
as well.

Grandma stepped outside the arena and leaned against the
top rail of the fence, raising a hand to her forehead to shield
her eyes from the sun. "Walk her around and let her stretch her
legs for a few minutes. Then let me see a nice slow jog."

Rosie squeezed lightly with her heels, and leaned forward to pet the pony's neck. "I love you, Jet!"

"Sit up straight," Grandma called out.

Rosie sat up and looked ahead through Jet's short, fuzzy ears, listening for her grandmother's next instructions.

After Grandma ran Rosie through several schooling exercises, she nodded approvingly. "You're doing very well. I'll be right back. I'm going to get Kezzie saddled."

"Okay." Rosie signaled Jet to trot. She broke into a song as they trotted around the ring. The pony's ears flicked back and forth, listening to her rider's slightly off-key voice.

Soon Grandma reappeared, leading her chestnut mare toward the arena. "Let's ride in the woods." She waved her hand in front of her face. "I don't know about you, but I think Jet's had enough of this dust."

Rosie loved any kind of riding, but she especially liked it when she was allowed to leave the arena and ride around the property of Sonrise Stable. Jet whinnied a greeting to her friend, Kezzie. Rosie envied the horses' friendship. Someday she hoped to have a best friend too.

Grandma opened the arena gate for Rosie, then mounted Kezzie. They rode the horses at a walk past the barn, across the pasture, and into the woods.

"Fall is my favorite time of year," Grandma said. "Don't you love the sound of the horses crunching through the leaves?"

"What? I can't hear you," Rosie shouted. "The leaves are making too much noise!"

"Whoa." Grandma pulled back on the reins, and Kezzie stopped. She turned the horse around to face Rosie. "Those leaves against Jet's black coat would make a beautiful picture. I wish I had brought my camera."

Rosie leaned over, laughing as she tried to catch the multicolored leaves spiraling down from the trees. "It's snowing leaves!"

Jet stopped when she felt her rider's weight shift in the saddle. The pony stood patiently, leaves swirling around her, and waited for Rosie to reposition herself.

"You silly girl." Grandma smiled. "It's a good thing that pony knows how to take care of you, otherwise you'd probably land on your head."

"Jet won't let me fall off," Rosie said. "It's not that far to the ground anyway."

"Come on, you two." Grandma waved Rosie forward.

Rosie urged her pony into a trot to catch up. When she got close enough, Jet gave Kezzie a playful nip on the hindquarters. The chestnut mare squealed and stomped her foot as a warning to the mischievous pony. Although she was much smaller, Jet didn't seem to realize it. She loved to be the leader and was not intimidated by trail obstacles that often frightened larger horses.

Rosie and her grandmother rode side by side along the trail, rocking gently to the horses' rhythm.

"This is the kind of riding I love. No horse shows or competitions—just taking it easy, enjoying my horse and the beauty of God's creation."

The breeze flipped a section of Kezzie's long, flaxen mane over her neck. Grandma reached down and moved the hair back to the correct side. "Sometimes it seems like only yesterday that I began training her. Good horses are rare, and she's been a great one."

"But she's not as good as Jet," Rosie insisted.

"Maybe not, but almost." Grandma paused with a mysterious smile on her face. "Next year, I'll have another training project. You're learning so quickly; I think you'll be ready to help me."

Rosie tilted her head and looked up at her grandmother. "Me? Train a horse? How could I do that? I'm not that good yet."

"Not exactly a horse. A foal."

"A foal?" Rosie repeated, still not understanding.

"Yes. Jet's foal."

As the meaning of her grandmother's words sank in, Rosie nearly bounced off the pony. "A foal? Jet's going to have a baby? When?"

Grandma smiled at Rosie's reaction.

"Oh, no! Am I hurting her?" Rosie stood in the stirrups. "Should I be riding her now?"

"Calm down. She's not going to have it tomorrow! It takes horses eleven months to have a foal."

"Oh." Rosie gently sat down and tried to calculate when eleven months would be.

"You can keep riding Jet for a while. The exercise will be good for her. She won't have the foal until early next spring."

When they returned to the barn, Rosie helped her grandmother removed the saddle, then she ran a brush lightly over the pony's side.

"She won't break. You can groom her like you always have."

Next, Rosie dumped a wheelbarrow full of fresh shavings into Jet's stall. "This will make a nice, soft bed for you."

The pony pawed at the pile of shavings.

"I know you like to arrange it yourself. That's why I didn't spread them out." Rosie moved the wheelbarrow into the aisle, then stood by the open stall door watching the pony paw the shavings around until she was satisfied with the arrangement.

Rosie dumped Jet's water bucket outside the barn and refilled it, then put a flake of grass hay in the rack. "Is there anything else I should do, Grandma?"

"That's everything for now. We can ride again this evening if you want to."

"Of course!" Rosie slipped her small, soft hand into Grandma's strong one, and they walked toward the house together.

Rosie spent most of the next three days at the barn with her grandmother and the horses. She wished every day could be like that, but her brief vacation soon came to an end. When her mother returned, Rosie eagerly told her the news about Jet.

Kristy looked surprised. "Why didn't you tell me, Mom? There haven't been any foals at Sonrise Stable since Ebony had Jet."

"I just found out last week for sure and wanted Rosie to be the first to know."

"It's a good thing we homeschool, Rosie. If you work hard and finish your work early, we'll come out twice a week now so you can ride and help Grandma with Jet and Kezzie."

"I will, Mom," Rosie promised. "Grandma needs my help."

And Rosie kept her word.

Kristy suggested that maybe Jet should have a foal every year, if it would motivate Rosie to do so well with her schoolwork.

The days shortened and grew increasingly crisp and cool as winter approached. The trees were bare now, having long ago shed their leaves. Everything was a dull, drab brown, except for a few green pines—reminders that spring and new life would come again.

With the cold weather, Rosie wasn't riding as much, but she still enjoyed spending time with her pony. Rosie shivered as she and her grandmother walked to the barn one particularly cold day.

"Don't you have a heavier coat?"

Rosie nodded. "I didn't think it would be this cold." She crossed her arms tightly, her teeth chattering. When they reached the barn, she slid Jet's stall door open. "She looks bigger."

"You've been feeding her too many carrots, haven't you?"

Rosie jerked her head toward the pony, then looked back at Grandma. It dawned on her that her grandmother was joking. "I better not feed her quite so many—just in case."

"We'll have to be careful about her diet," Grandma agreed. "We don't want her to gain too much weight too soon."

Rosie watched the pony chew her hay. "I still can't believe Jet's going to have a foal!"

3

Christmas in the Barn

꒦

Rosie perched beside her grandmother on the bottom row of a stack of hay bales in the barn. The mid-December day was so cold she shivered inside her heavy winter coat. She moved closer to Grandma and pulled Jemimah, the calico barn cat, onto her lap. The cat burrowed under Rosie's coat creating something like a feline furnace.

"What are we doing, Grandma? Can I give Jet her present now?" Even though it wasn't Christmas yet, Rosie couldn't resist bringing her pony an early gift. Her grandmother had insisted that she leave it in the tack room until later.

"In a few minutes." Grandma reached into her coat pocket and pulled out a small New Testament. She turned to Luke's gospel and began to read the Christmas story.

"And it came to pass in those days, that there went out a decree from Caesar Augustus, that all the world should be taxed—"

Rosie stared at the small, foggy clouds that formed as Grandma's breath encountered the zero-degree temperature.

Kezzie and Jet munched hay in their stalls, occasionally looking over as if they were listening to the story.

"I've never heard of anyone reading the Bible in a barn." The wind whistled fiercely outside. Rosie put her arms around the bulge of cat inside her coat and scooted closer to her grandmother.

"I started doing this at Christmas when your mom was about your age. Of course you remember that Christ was born in a stable—"

"Because there was no room in the inn," Rosie added. "And He was laid in a manger—a feed box."

Grandma nodded and resumed reading. "And so it was, that, while they were there, the days were accomplished that she should be delivered. And she brought forth her firstborn son, and wrapped him in swaddling clothes, and laid him in a manger; because there was no room for them in the inn."

Rosie fidgeted as she listened. As soon as her grandmother finished the story, she leaped off the hay bale. "Ow!" She reached inside her coat and carefully detached Jemimah's claws from the top of her leg.

"Sorry, Jemimah! I forgot you were in there. I have to give Jet her Christmas present now." The cat climbed up higher in the stacked hay, and Rosie disappeared for a moment, returning with a red stocking stuffed full of carrots. She tied it to the hanger on the front of Jet's stall and stepped back to watch.

Jet heard Rosie and popped her head over the door to investigate. She nuzzled the fuzzy stocking, wiggling it until she got her teeth around one of the carrots. The pony pulled a large carrot out and crunched into it while Kezzie looked on enviously.

"Where's my horse's gift?" Grandma protested.

"I guess Kezzie can have one. Just one." Rosie pawed around to find the smallest carrot and fed it to Kezzie. The horse bobbed her head as she ate.

When Jet finished her last carrot, she grabbed the stocking between her teeth. The pony shook her head up and down and pulled the stocking off its hook.

"No, girl!" Rosie ran to the door, but Jet disappeared into the back of her stall. "Grandma, if she eats the stocking, she'll get sick!"

Grandma hurried into the stall. "Jet, you give me that. Right now!" She pulled, but the pony clenched her teeth and pulled back.

Rosie heard a ripping sound. "Oh, Jet!"

Grandma grabbed the pony's halter, stood at her side, and pried the stocking out of Jet's mouth. She held it in front of her with the tips of her fingers and handed it to Rosie.

With her gloved hand, Rosie tried to brush bits of partially chewed hay and carrot from the soggy, torn stocking. "Jet, you bad girl! You ruined your Christmas present." She frowned at the pony, who tossed her head.

Jet didn't seem at all remorseful about tearing the stocking, only angry that Grandma had taken it away from her.

Rosie set the stocking down on the tack box. "Grandma, when will I get to ride her again? If she was getting more exercise maybe she wouldn't be so naughty."

Grandma sat on a bale and leaned back against the hay. "If only I had an indoor arena. I've always wanted one, but they're so expensive. As cold as it gets around here, it's difficult to ride all year without one."

"Cold like today!" Rosie jumped up and down in the barn aisle doing a few jumping jacks to warm herself.

"In the spring, Jet will be too close to her foaling date, but you'll have plenty of time to ride next summer, after the foal is born." Grandma placed her hand on Rosie's shoulder. "I think you'll be ready for your first horse show then."

Rosie's eyes widened. "Really? Now I have two things to wait for—the foal and my first horse show. I don't know if I can stand it!"

"I know what you mean," Grandma laughed. "I'm almost as excited as you are. Now, let's go back to the house. How does a big cup of hot chocolate sound?" She patted her gloved hands together. "I can't feel my fingertips anymore. The problem with reading the Christmas story in the barn is that it's freezing out here!"

Rosie gave Jet a quick kiss, then walked out the door with her grandmother. "I'll race you to the house!"

Grandma counted, "One, two, three—go!" She stomped her foot on "go," and Rosie took off like a shot.

Rosie was halfway to the house when she paused to look back. What? Grandma wasn't running at all. She'd barely even left the barn.

An eerie sound filled the cold winter air. *Yip, yip, yip, ar, ar, arrrrrrrrr...*

Rosie gulped and turned slowly, looking all around her. She ran back to her grandmother and pressed close to her side. "Wha—What was that?"

Grandma cocked her head as she listened to the haunting sound. "Sounds like coyotes—or maybe a pack of wild dogs."

Rosie noticed the worried look on her grandmother's face. "Where are they?"

"I don't know for sure, but it sounded like it was coming from the woods. Let's hurry and get inside." Grandma grabbed Rosie's hand and walked briskly toward the house.

4
The Storm

❧

March blew in, with glimpses of the spring that would soon follow. Kezzie and Jet grew restless after being cooped up in the barn all winter. When it wasn't raining or snowing, Grandma hooked their back stall doors open so they could go out to the pasture for fresh air and exercise.

On her next visit to Sonrise Stable, Rosie ran to look into her pony's stall. "You are so fat, Jet! Grandma, I think she's ready to have her foal right now."

The pony still had a full winter coat, which exaggerated her roundness. As Jet turned to face them, Rosie could see her abdomen bulging on both sides as if she carried twins. The pony didn't seem concerned about the loss of her slim figure. She stared at Rosie, waiting for a treat.

"While you've been on vacation the past few weeks, Jet's been busy eating. The foal's not due for another month, but she is very plump, isn't she?"

Rosie couldn't wait for the foal to be born. She entered the stall and squeezed Jet's neck. She walked around the pony, marveling at how much bigger she looked since she had last seen her. "Did you miss me, chubby girl?"

"I've started checking on her several times a day now and once in the middle of the night," Grandma said. "I wish your grandfather were still alive. He was never much for riding, but he loved taking care of the horses." Grandma covered her mouth, fighting unsuccessfully to stifle a yawn. "I could use his help now. I can't seem to get enough sleep with this schedule."

Rosie wondered what it would be like if her grandfather were still alive. Her memory of him was formed mostly from old family photographs, since he had died when she was just a baby. Her dad's parents lived in another state, so she didn't see them often. "Aren't I a good helper, Grandma?"

"You're a great helper." Grandma patted her on the head. "I don't know how I'd take care of these animals without you."

After saying goodbye to her granddaughter that evening, Grandma sank onto the couch in front of the crackling fireplace. She stared at the flames and smiled—Rosie was the spitting image of her middle daughter, Kristy, when she was that age. It would be fun to work with the foal together with Rosie, and the girl would learn so much about training a horse by starting with the basics.

Grandma tried to keep her eyes open, but between getting up in the middle of the night all week and the warmth of the fire, she drifted into a deep sleep. Two hours later, she woke with the uneasy feeling that something was wrong at the barn. Hurrying to the laundry room, she jammed her feet into a pair of boots and pulled on a coat, hat, and gloves. She grabbed a flashlight from the shelf.

The wind nearly yanked the door out of her hand as she stepped outside. Icy rain pelted her face. She shivered and drew her coat more tightly around her. The beam of the flashlight bounced crazily on the path as she slipped and slid through several inches of new fallen snow crusted over with ice.

A banging sound alarmed her as she approached the barn. Grandma caught her breath when she saw the rear door of Jet's stall swinging back and forth in the strong wind. *What? I'm sure I fastened that this afternoon!*

Inside, Kezzie pranced nervously in her stall. Where was Jet? Grandma frantically searched the barn, but there was no sign of the pony.

"Don't worry, Kezzie." Grandma paused briefly to pat her horse's forehead. "I'll find your little friend." She walked out the back of Jet's stall into the pasture. The darkness was so thick she could barely see ten feet in front of her.

Grandma tramped through the snow to the center of the field. Holding the flashlight in one hand and shielding her eyes from the stinging, icy pellets with the other, she turned slowly around. The beam of light only revealed more snow and ice. "Jet, where are you? Come on, girl; it's cold out here. Let's get you back into the barn!"

Grandma continued on. When she reached the woods, the trees provided shelter from the wind and icy rain, but it was darker than ever.

She tripped over a root and threw her hands forward to catch herself. The flashlight sailed through the air and landed with a thud followed by pitch-blackness.

"Ow!" Grandma winced and rubbed her hands together. Rising to her knees, she crawled, patting the ground around her until her hand bumped into the light. She picked it up and flipped the switch, but nothing happened.

"Come on." She hit the flashlight against the palm of her hand a few times. The light flickered and finally stayed on. A branch cracked to her right. Whirling around, she aimed the flashlight in that direction. Squinting, she tried to make her eyes focus in the darkness. Something moved in the distance—a shadowy shape too small to be Jet. *A coyote?*

She stood, nearly frozen with fear, then took a few halting steps backward. Switching the flashlight over to her left hand, she bent down, never taking her eyes off the animal. A short, thick stick poked up out of the snow. She grabbed it and shook the snow off. The stick wasn't much, but it was all the protection she had. She squeezed it tightly and backed up again. The animal seemed to be stalking her, slowly moving closer and closer.

Grandma stepped behind the nearest tree and peeked out, straining to see what was approaching. She glanced up to see how high the closest branch was. A coyote wouldn't be able to climb a tree, but she wasn't sure she could either.

As she watched and waited, it became clear that the animal wasn't stalking her at all, just wandering aimlessly in the snow. When it stepped out from a cluster of trees into a small clearing, Grandma gasped. "Oh, no!" She released her grip on the stick, and it fell to the ground. She switched the flashlight back to her right hand and aimed the beam straight ahead.

The foal? How could that be? It's too soon. But that's what stood before her, struggling to maintain its balance on the icy ground. *Where was Jet? She would never leave her baby.* Grandma could feel the fear rising in her throat. She went to search in the direction the foal had come from. Her heart sank when she found Jet, lying strangely still in the snow.

"No!" Grandma yelled and snapped the light off for a moment. Her knees suddenly felt so weak, she was afraid she might fall. Tears filled her eyes and spilled down her cheeks. "What happened?"

Moving closer, she discovered a second lifeless form—a dog, or coyote, apparently trampled to death. She sank down into the snow beside the pony and stroked her neck. "Oh, Jet, you were protecting your little one, weren't you? I knew you would be a good mother."

She would have stayed there beside Jet, crying, but she could see the foal shivering in the cold wind. Born a month early, the baby was mostly legs. Grandma stood and scooped it up in her arms, pressing her head firmly against the foal's neck. She closed her eyes. *Was she too late to save this little one? Why had she let herself fall asleep in front of the fire?*

5
Scamper

With her arms wrapped tightly around the foal, Grandma struggled to keep the flashlight focused on the ground ahead of her feet. She didn't want to trip over something in the dark again. Her arms and shoulders soon began to ache. Ignoring the pain, she didn't stop until she reached the back of the barn. Grandma leaned against the sliding door for a moment to catch her breath. The foal was quiet in her arms. She hoped it was still alive. Nudging the door with her foot, she slid it open far enough to walk through. Once inside, she headed straight to the tack room, kicking the door shut behind her. Her arms were stiff, as if they were locked around the foal. She leaned over and forced them to release their grip, gently setting the foal down on the wood floor.

When she flicked the light switch on, she had her first good look at Jet's baby—a handsome black-and-white colt. "Oh, you're beautiful." She pulled two towels from the foaling kit prepared weeks earlier and rubbed the colt's coat to warm him.

To help hold in his body heat, she draped one of the towels over him like a horse blanket.

From her experience raising Kezzie years before, Grandma knew the foal needed milk soon. She reached for the barn phone. Between her nerves and the cold, it was difficult to make her fingers work properly. Finally she was able to punch in the correct numbers. After she had spoken with her veterinarian, Dr. Rings, she leaned back against the wall and slowly slid down to the floor. She prayed that the vet would arrive soon. Then it was just a matter of waiting.

The foal folded his spindly legs and dropped down next to her. Grandma wrapped her arm around him and pulled his head onto her lap, stroking his soft coat. Now that she had time to think, her tears started again and dropped onto the foal's neck. Time seemed to drag by like a movie played in slow motion. She checked her watch every few minutes. *Why isn't Dr. Rings here?*

Grandma stood and began to dial the vet's number again, but she was interrupted by a vehicle honking outside. "She's here." She held out her hand to the foal. "You stay put. I'll be right back."

"I'm so sorry about Jet," Dr. Rings said after Grandma explained what had happened. "Let's see what we can do for this little guy." She went out to her truck and returned with a large plastic bottle and a bag of powdered milk. Grandma moved the foal into the barn aisle where there was more room.

It only took a little coaxing before the hungry foal discovered how to drink the replacement milk from the bottle. When his tummy was full, he looked up at them with white, milky foam covering his tiny muzzle. His large brown eyes seemed to ask, *What now?*

"Okay, little fellow, let's move you into your new home."
Grandma put one hand under his head and pulled, while the
vet pushed gently on his hindquarters. They guided him into a
clean stall with a fluffy bed of fresh straw.

Grandma hung a heat lamp in one corner, out of the foal's
reach, to provide extra warmth. Kezzie, in the adjoining stall,
seemed puzzled. Pushing her head over the divider, she stared
at her new neighbor as if to say, *Who are you? And where is
my buddy, Jet?* She made a loud, snuffly sound through her
nostrils, which sent the foal scampering around his stall.

Despite her sadness and fatigue, Grandma smiled at the
foal's antics. "Scamper. That's a good name for you."

She suddenly remembered Rosie, and an incredible pain
washed over her. "Oh God, I don't understand this myself. How
will I explain it to my granddaughter?"

Grandma stood watching the foal long after Dr. Rings had left. Finally, she trudged back through the snow to the house where she gathered a cot, a sleeping bag, and an electric heater. She returned to the barn and set up camp in the tack room.

The vet had stressed the importance of offering the foal milk frequently during the first week, to imitate the nursing pattern he would have had with his mother. Grandma set her watch to alert her every hour throughout the night so she could check on Scamper and see whether he wanted his bottle. She settled in and managed to get some sleep before the next feeding.

Early the next morning, Grandma rolled over on the cot, exhausted. *What was that noise? It sounded like an airplane.* She pushed herself up and listened, forcing her eyes to remain open. Was it only a dream? As her mind cleared, she realized it was the sound of the big front door of the barn sliding open. She stumbled to the door of the tack room, opened it, and leaned out. Her eyes blinked rapidly as they adjusted to the light.

"Grandma?"

"Rosie?" Grandma blinked again. "Kristy? What are you doing here?"

"Mom? You scared me! I didn't expect to see you at the barn this early." Kristy walked down the aisle toward the tack room. "Rosie said you were tired from checking on Jet overnight, so I thought we'd come and cover the morning shift for you."

"Mom! Mom!" Rosie shrieked. "Jet had her foal! Come and see!" She started to run toward her mother, then turned and went back to the foal's stall.

"Grandma, where's Jet? Why isn't she with her baby?" Rosie opened the stall door. She placed one arm around Scamper's neck and stroked his forehead with the other. The foal found one of her fingers and began to suck, thinking he had found his breakfast. Rosie laughed with delight. "He's trying to eat my finger!"

Grandma walked over and wearily sat down on the tack box, tears streaming down her cheeks. She took a deep breath and slowly let it out. "Rosie, would you come here for a minute?"

"Aw, but I want to play with the baby." Rosie reluctantly stepped out of the stall, gently pushing the foal back enough so she could close the door. She looked in the stall to the left of Scamper's. "Where is Jet?"

Grandma patted the tack box, motioning for Rosie to sit beside her. Kristy sat on the other end. As Grandma explained the events of the night before, all three held each other and cried.

Finally, Rosie was able to speak. "Why, Grandma? Why did my pony have to die? It's not fair."

Grandma brushed away more tears. *Would they never end?* She had cried so much the night before, she couldn't believe she had any tears left. "Rosie, I won't pretend to understand why this happened. But I know God can use the painful things in our lives for good."

Grandma closed her eyes briefly and silently prayed for words that would help Rosie understand. "The Bible says that God knows when a sparrow falls to the ground. God created

Jet, and He loved her as much, or more, than you and I did. You know the verse John 3:16[1], right?"

Rosie nodded slowly. Jemimah jumped into her lap, and she absently stroked the cat's head.

"When it says 'God gave His only Son,' it's talking about when Jesus came and lived as a man on earth."

Rosie's tears slowed, but Grandma sensed she had no idea what this had to do with Jet.

"Jesus died on the cross to pay the penalty for our sins. He gave His life for ours, so we could have eternal life. Why would He do that for us?"

Rosie shrugged.

"That's what the 'For God so loved the world' part of the verse is about. Jesus came because of God's amazing love for us."

Grandma continued. "The animal that attacked Jet was what some people call a coydog, part coyote and part dog, probably starving after the hard winter. Being part dog, they are less fearful than coyotes. Since the foal was weak and helpless, it probably went after him first. When Jet tried to protect her foal, it attacked her. Do you see now? Jet loved her baby so much; she gave her life so he could live."

"It's not exactly the same, of course," Grandma added. "But what Jet did for her foal helps me understand what Jesus did for me—for all of us."

Grandma watched Rosie turn this over in her mind.

"I kind of understand, but it doesn't make me feel any better."

---

1   For God so loved the world, that he gave his only begotten Son, that whosoever believeth in him should not perish, but have everlasting life.

"I know. It will hurt for a long time." Grandma nodded sadly. "Jet made many children happy by teaching them how to ride. Maybe someday the story of her death can do something even better if it helps them understand what Christ did for us on the cross."

"I don't think I could tell anyone about it," Rosie said slowly.

"It will take time." They sat together quietly for several minutes, then Grandma broke the silence by blowing her nose on a damp wad of tissues retrieved from her coat pocket. "I named him Scamper. He needs to be fed every two hours for the next few days. Will you help me take care of him?"

Rosie shrugged. "I guess so."

"You can stay here with Grandma for a few days," Kristy offered. "I mean—if you feel up to it."

Grandma stood up, feeling her age for the first time in her life. Her back ached as she returned to the tack room for Scamper's bottle. After cleaning it and mixing a fresh batch of milk, she held it out to her granddaughter.

Rosie sniffed and raised her hand to take the bottle. "What do I do with it?"

"He knows what to do," Grandma said.

Rosie nudged Jemimah off her lap and shuffled toward the stall. Grandma slid the door open. Scamper butted the bottle and eagerly began to drink.

"Tip it up so the milk comes out more easily," Grandma said.

Rosie smiled briefly through her tears as the hungry little colt energetically attacked the bottle she held with both hands.

Over the next few months, Rosie and Grandma spent many hours at the barn caring for Scamper. Each day the time between his feedings was gradually extended. As he grew stronger, they taught him to drink his milk from a bucket instead of the bottle. He also began to nibble at small bits of hay and grain.

Jet was buried in the back pasture beside her mother, Ebony. Rosie and Grandma remembered with sadness and joy the pony they had loved so dearly.

6
Early Training

G randma, he looks so funny." Rosie laughed at Scamper,
who had a jacket draped over his back. "Why did you
put your coat on him?"

"I've never seen it in any horse-training book, but I did this
kind of thing when I trained Kezzie years ago. One day he'll be
asked to carry a rider—"

"Me!" Rosie grinned.

Grandma nodded. "If he becomes accustomed to carrying
things now, a saddle won't be a big deal to him when he's
grown up." She removed the jacket and held it near Scamper's
nose. The foal sniffed it all over and then blew out of his
nostrils.

"Here, assistant trainer." Grandma held the jacket out to
Rosie. "Take this and rub it all over him."

Rosie took the jacket. She loved the idea of being a horse
trainer. Maybe someday she really would be one, like her aunt,
Julie. She let the heavy fabric flop over Scamper's neck, back,
and down his legs.

"That's it," Grandma encouraged her. "He needs to get used to being touched all over by people and objects so he won't be afraid of saddle straps or actions like a rider removing a coat."

Rosie looked into Scamper's eyes. The colt seemed puzzled by this new development, but he wasn't afraid. He stood quietly in the aisle while they worked with him. Over the past three months, he had grown to trust Grandma and Rosie completely.

Rosie paused and absently stroked Scamper's neck. She was surprised to feel her eyes fill and a tear spill over and drip down her cheek. Would she ever stop crying about Jet? She quickly wiped her eye, not wanting Grandma to notice, but nothing seemed to escape her grandmother's attention.

"What's wrong?"

"Oh Grandma." Rosie sniffed. "I love Scamper, but sometimes he reminds me so much of Jet that it makes me sad. I miss her so much."

Grandma pulled a tissue from her pocket and handed it to Rosie. "Yes. That's a night I wish I could forget. But when I feel sad, I try to replace the bad thoughts with happy ones."

Rosie draped the jacket over Scamper's back again. "How do you do that?"

"By remembering. You were too young to remember this, but the first time you rode Jet—you must have been about two—I led the pony and your mom and dad walked on either side of her. You held onto that saddle horn for dear life, but you had the biggest grin on your face. That's when I knew we had another cowgirl in the family."

Rosie ran her fingers through Scamper's soft mane as she listened. The foal's hair was growing, but it wasn't long enough to lie over yet. His fluffy black mane stood straight up.

"Remember when she grabbed the carrots out of her Christmas stocking?"

"And nearly ate the stocking!" Grandma smiled and nodded. "My favorite memory is that time we rode together last fall—with the leaves swirling around you two. I can see it clearly in my mind. I wish I had taken a photo then."

"I could draw a picture of that for you." Rosie loved to draw, and she was getting quite good at drawing her favorite animal.

Grandma smiled. "That would be great! Thank—"

"Hey!" Rosie turned suddenly toward the foal. "What are you doing?"

Scamper had pulled the jacket off his back and was chewing on one of the sleeves. Grandma carefully pried it out of his mouth.

"Just like his momma," Rosie said, "part billy goat."

Grandma scratched Scamper's neck and hugged him. "He's a good boy for his age. Because he's an orphan and has spent so much time with us, Kezzie has to remind him nearly every day that he's a horse, not a human. She's made it clear that she's first in the pecking order."

Kezzie put her head over her stall door and nickered. Grandma laughed. "See. She agrees with me."

A picture of Kezzie pecking Scamper came to Rosie's mind, and she laughed. "Pecking order? She's a horse not a chicken."

"You watch sometime when I feed them together, and you'll see Kezzie's version of pecking. In a herd, the boss is usually a mare. She's called the lead mare. Each of the other horses in the herd will have their order after her. The lead mare gets to eat first, drink first, and stand wherever she wants. All the horses get out of her way when she moves around."

"That sounds selfish. Mom always tells me to put Jesus first, then Others, then Yourself. She says that's what gives us JOY."

"Your mom's right," Grandma agreed. "The pecking order is important for horses in the wild, but it doesn't work well for people. The respect the other horses have for the lead mare causes them to obey her without stopping to think. She's always on the lookout and alerts the herd when she senses danger. So she has responsibilities along with her privileges."

Grandma continued working around Scamper, running her hand down his legs and picking up each hoof briefly. "Why don't you grab a lead rope and get Kezzie? We'll take them out to the arena and work on their ground manners."

"Are you going to teach him to say please and thank you?" Rosie respected her grandmother's knowledge and enjoyed learning new things from her about horses, but she had also picked up a little of her grandmother's sense of humor.

"It's very similar to that, actually. Scamper needs to learn to listen to and obey people. There are some things we can teach him while he's young—like being led with a loose lead. He shouldn't barge ahead and drag his handler or lag behind so he has to be pulled along. I'll also teach him to turn whenever I turn, back up, and always keep a safe amount of space between us. At three months, he's too small to do much damage, but imagine when he weighs nine hundred pounds. You wouldn't want him stepping on your foot then, would you?"

"No! Please teach him his ground manners!" Rosie hopped up and down on one foot while holding the other, grimacing with imaginary pain. She remembered how much it had hurt when Jet, who wasn't a very big pony, had stepped on her foot once.

Rosie ran to the tack room and picked up a lead rope. Jet's saddle caught her eye. It looked sad and lonely sitting on a rack in the corner. She fingered the bracelet on her left wrist and felt the tears starting again.

After Jet's death, Grandma had saved some of the pony's tail hair and had matching bracelets made for the two of them. The black, glossy hair had been braided and a silver cross attached at one end. *God, I'll never forget my pony, Jet, but thank you for Scamper. Please help me do a good job helping Grandma train him.*

Rosie hurried to Kezzie's stall. She was continuing her lessons on her grandmother's horse until Scamper was old enough to ride. When she slid the door open, the chestnut mare came to her, lowered her head to Rosie's level, and sniffed.

41

Rosie put her arms around the horse's neck and squeezed. "I'm glad I have you to ride, old girl." She snapped the rope on Kezzie's halter, led her down the aisle, and followed Grandma and Scamper out of the barn.

Grandma stopped when they reached the middle of the arena. "You work with Kezzie, while I work with this little guy. She'll be a good example for him."

They spent the next fifteen minutes leading the horses, practicing stops, starts, turns, and backing, then Grandma announced that they had done enough for one day. "At his age, he has a short attention span. It's important to stop on a positive note."

They put Scamper and Kezzie back in their stalls. "You can stay here a while longer and brush him while I go fix us a snack. Double-check that his door is latched before you leave the barn." Grandma had changed the style of locks on the stall doors after Jet's escape so that none of the horses could get out.

Rosie reached for a rubber currycomb and curried Scamper vigorously under his neck, causing him to stretch his head forward as Jet used to do. "You like this, don't you, boy?"

Switching over, she curried the other side, then picked up a body brush. She enjoyed spending time in the barn with the horses. The previous summer she had overheard someone at the county fair complaining about the smell in the horse barn. That didn't make sense to her. She loved everything about her grandmother's barn: the worn and faded boards, the smells—leather, grain, and the hay stacked in the hayloft. But most of all, she loved the smell of the horses themselves.

Scamper turned and extended his head toward Rosie. She blew gently on his nose and waited until he blew softly back. She liked the sweet scent of his breath and imagined this was a secret language they shared. Rosie began to sing to him, daydreaming about the two of them taking first place in the jumper class at the fair some day. Scamper's eyes blinked, and his head drooped as he began to doze.

"Hi! Whatcha doing?"

Scamper jumped sideways. Rosie dropped the brush and whirled around to see a thin, blond girl about her own age standing in the barn aisle just outside the stall. "You shouldn't scare people like that!"

Rosie stroked Scamper's neck to calm him. Who was this girl?

7

Carrie

The girl, who seemed to have appeared out of nowhere, peeked through the partially open stall door. "I'm Carrie. I live over there." She pointed roughly in the direction of the pasture to the left of the barn.

That was odd. Rosie didn't remember ever seeing any kids at the neighbor's house. "I'm Rosie."

"When I got off the school bus, I saw you out front with the horses. Why don't you go to school?"

"I don't *go* anywhere to school. I'm homeschooled." Rosie was still annoyed that the girl had startled her and Scamper.

"I wish I was homeschooled. My school is boring." Carrie looked around the barn. "Where's your mom? I saw her helping you with the horses."

"That wasn't my mom," Rosie shook her head. "That's my grandmother."

Carrie frowned. "Oh. I don't have a mom either."

"No! I didn't mean that!" Rosie quickly explained. "I do have a mom. I just come to my grandmother's a lot. She's teaching me how to ride."

"Where's your grandmother then?"

"She went inside to fix something to eat." Rosie realized she had lost track of the time. She had no idea how long she'd been at the barn. "Grandma probably wonders where I am. I should go over to the house now."

Carrie walked into the stall and stood beside Scamper. "Could I ride him?"

Rosie's eyes grew wide. "Of course not! He's only a few months old. No one can ride him for a couple more years."

"What about that horse?" Carrie nodded toward Kezzie in the next stall. "Could I ride that one?"

Rosie began picking up the brushes she had used on Scamper. "That's my grandmother's horse. We're not allowed to ride her unless my grandma is out here." She didn't want to be rude, but she wished Carrie would go back to her house. She dropped the last brush into the tack bucket, stepped out of Scamper's stall, and motioned for Carrie to follow her. When they were both in the aisle, she closed and latched Scamper's door.

Carrie crossed her arms and stared at Rosie. "You're just afraid to ride her."

"Kezzie?" Rosie put her hands on her hips and glared. Why was this girl being so rude? "I am not afraid. I've ridden her lots of times."

"Let me see you get on her then."

Rosie hesitated. "I'm not allowed to, because my grandma isn't here."

"You're a scaredy-cat! You'll be afraid to ride that little one when he's older too." Carrie pointed toward Scamper.

Rosie could feel her face growing hot and knew it was turning bright red. "I'll show you. Just watch this." She stomped into Kezzie's stall, climbed the boards of the side wall, and leaped onto the horse's back. Kezzie slowly turned her head and stared at her small rider.

"Rosalyn Marie!" Grandma's voice thundered from the front of the barn.

Oh no. Rosie steadied herself on Kezzie's back and turned to see her grandmother marching down the aisle.

"What in the world are you doing?"

Carrie stood frozen for a moment. "Uh, I th-think someone's calling me."

Grandma pointed a finger at her. "You wait just a minute, young lady."

Carrie bolted past her, and ran out the front door.

Grandma stepped into the stall. "You know you're never to be on the horses unless I'm out here. You don't even have a halter or bridle on Kezzie! That wasn't a very smart thing to do."

Rosie hung her head as her grandmother helped her down. Grandma walked across the aisle and sat on the tack box. "Sit down and tell me what happened. Who was that girl, anyway?"

Rosie was too worked up to sit down. She paced back and forth in front of her grandmother. "She said she lives next door. Her name is Carrie. I was mad because she said I was afraid to ride Kezzie. She called me a scaredy-cat."

"Hmm, I didn't know there were any children next door."

47

"I wanted to show her I wasn't afraid. Grandma, I'm sorry. I knew I shouldn't do it, but I couldn't stop myself."

"At least you're not blaming someone else for what you did wrong." Grandma's voice softened. "I'll have to talk to your mom and dad about this. A couple weeks away from the horses should help you remember to do the right thing next time."

Rosie couldn't believe what she had heard. Weeks away from Kezzie and Scamper? That didn't seem fair!

"When I was your age, I used to have a problem with letting other people talk me into doing things."

"Really?" Rosie sat beside her grandmother.

"Yes. Let's see. . . Candy was my neighbor and best friend. She and I always had a great time riding our ponies, Frosty and Dolly, together. One summer afternoon, Candy and Frosty came over. We were standing by our front door talking, when all of a sudden, I saw a sparkle in Candy's eye, and a big grin spread across her face.

"She looked at the door and then back at me. 'I bet Frosty would go into your house.' I didn't doubt that. Frosty was the kind of pony you could do anything with. We often had three of us kids riding him at once. When he got tired, he would head for the closest tree. If we didn't jump down quickly, he would take us under a branch and help us off.

"I shook my head at Candy and said, 'I don't think that's a good idea.' My mom was inside, and I was certain that she would not appreciate a pony in our house. But Candy challenged me, 'I guess you're scared to try it.'

"'Scared? Me?'" Grandma shook her head. "I remember I held out both hands and said, 'Give me that rope.'

"Candy handed over Frosty's lead and opened the door while I steered that chubby little pony through. Once inside, Frosty glanced around and seemed to smile—as if he felt right at home. We traveled through the kitchen and into the dining room. A left turn brought us into the living room where my mom was relaxing in a recliner, absorbed in a book.

"Maybe it was the sound of Frosty's hooves clip-clopping on the hardwood floor or Candy and I giggling—something got my mother's attention. She peered over the top of her book and then jumped straight up in the air. I'd never seen such a look on her face. When she was able to speak, she yelled, 'Viiicki, get that pony out of here—NOW!'"

Grandma laughed. "The three of us didn't waste any time leaving! It's a good thing Frosty didn't use the bathroom during his visit. I can't imagine what my punishment would have been then."

Rosie giggled. "Did you really do that, Grandma?"

"Yes, Rosie, I did. It's a funny story, but it shows how easily I was persuaded to do something I shouldn't have. I was more concerned about what my friend thought of me than about doing what was right. Throughout your life, you'll always have people who will try to get you to do wrong things. You need to be strong enough to resist that pressure. The Bible says that bad company corrupts good character.[1] You need to be careful who you choose to be your friends and what kind of influence you allow them to have on you."

Was Carrie "bad company?" Rosie wasn't sure how you could tell, when you had just met someone. She remembered what good friends Jet and Kezzie had been. She wanted to have a close friend like that. "Do you think I shouldn't be friends with Carrie?"

Grandma pursed her lips. "Someone moved in that house a few weeks ago. I should have gone over to introduce myself before now. I'll do that this afternoon—and I'll invite Carrie over so we can get to know her better."

She patted Rosie's knee. "I hope you learned a lesson from this. Bad choices like that can have effects that last a lifetime. What if Kezzie had jumped and you had fallen off? You might have been seriously injured."

"I don't know how I'll be able to stand two weeks without seeing Scamper and Kezzie." Rosie's shoulders drooped as she slowly followed her grandmother out of the barn. "Couldn't you spank me instead?"

---

1   1 Corinthians 15:33

Grandma stopped. "No, it will be better to give you time to think it over. Scamper won't change much in two weeks, and then you can come back and work with him again."

Rosie sighed. "I'd still rather have a spanking."

8
Kezzie's Story

꙳

"Hi, Mrs. Watson." Carrie ran to join Grandma at the riding arena fence. She stuck her head through the rails and watched Rosie walk Kezzie over a wooden practice bridge.

Grandma greeted her and asked, "What do you think? Rosie's a good rider, isn't she?"

Carrie nodded without looking at Grandma. She had never ridden a horse before and was dying to ride Kezzie, but she was afraid to ask. Was Rosie's grandmother mad at her for daring Rosie to get on the horse?

Carrie had stopped over one day the previous week to see whether Rosie was there. Grandma had explained that Rosie was grounded from the horses for a while. Carrie felt bad for getting her in trouble.

It would be nice if they could be friends, but maybe Rosie was mad at her. It seemed she had a knack for saying or doing the wrong thing and getting herself—or someone else—in trouble. Carrie was normally shy, but in her previous foster home the other children had picked on her. She learned to be mean in order to protect herself.

Grandma smiled at her. "Would you like to learn how to ride Kezzie?"

Carrie's face lit up. "Me? Ride Kezzie?"

Grandma nodded.

"I've never ridden a horse before." Now that her dream was about to become reality, Carrie was a bit uncertain.

"I'll have to talk to your mother first. If it's okay with her, we can start tomorrow."

Carrie dug a hole in the dirt with her worn tennis shoe. "Mrs. Robinson isn't my mother." She hated explaining this to people. It made her feel more awkward than usual. People always gave her a funny look when they learned that she was a foster child.

Grandma raised her eyebrows. "She's not?"

"The Robinsons are my foster parents." Carrie leaned against the fence and sighed. "I don't know what happened to my real mom. No one tells me anything about her." She usually didn't like to talk to adults, but there was something about Rosie's grandmother that made her feel safe. She counted on the fingers of one hand. "This is the fifth foster home I can remember."

"Carrie, you won't be around me too long before you learn that I have a horse story for about every situation. Do you have a few minutes?"

Carrie nodded and followed Grandma to a picnic table under a big, shady maple tree.

Grandma called out to Rosie, "Walk her until she's cool, and then bring her over here." Turning back to Carrie, she began. "The horse Rosie is riding is Kezzie. She's been my horse for sixteen years. This story is about the night she was born. Her mother, Satin, was a black Tennessee Walking Horse that belonged to Rosie's mother.

"As Satin neared her time to foal, my girls and I took turns checking on her every few hours. One night I decided to go out earlier than my scheduled time. When I entered the barn, Satin was lying in her stall about to have her foal.

"My heart started pounding. For a moment, I couldn't make up my mind what to do. I wanted to stay at the barn, but I also wanted to let my husband and the girls know it was time. I knew the foal would be born any minute so I ran to the house and banged on the windows, yelling, 'Satin's having her foal!' It's a good thing we don't have close neighbors; I probably would have woken them up too. I made it back to the barn just in time to see the foal born."

"That was Kezzie, right?"

"I hadn't named her yet, but yes, that was Kezzie. Something didn't seem right though. Kezzie wasn't moving, and Satin didn't so much as sniff at her baby. I grabbed a cloth and cleared the foal's nostrils so she could breathe. She lay there so still and quiet; I began to wonder whether she was alive. But finally I saw her move."

Rosie rode up on Kezzie and joined them at the picnic table. She listened for a moment, then patted the horse's neck. "She's telling your story, girl."

Carrie wrinkled her forehead and looked at Grandma. "So Kezzie was all right after that?"

"Not exactly." Grandma returned to her story. "I took a towel and rubbed Kezzie all over until she was dry. She was so cute—reddish brown with a stripe down the middle of her forehead.

"She was determined to stand, but she couldn't get her long, spindly legs arranged well enough to maintain her balance. I hated to see her tumble over into the straw again and again. When she mastered it and was able to stand for the first time, we all cheered quietly. Then it struck me that Satin still showed no interest in her baby.

"It's important for foals to nurse soon after they're born, and Kezzie's instincts led her to seek out her mother. When her foal approached, Satin pinned her ears back and raised a hind leg as if to kick her. Each time Kezzie came near, Satin grew more aggressive. I hated to wake my vet at three o'clock in the morning, but I didn't know what else to do. Dr. Rings arrived an hour later and informed us, somewhat groggily, that it was her birthday too.

"After examining both of them, Dr. Rings gave Satin a tranquilizer to calm her so Kezzie could nurse. She left another shot and advised me to give Satin the second dose in a few hours if she was still aggressive toward the foal.

"Kristy and I spent the next several hours sitting in the barn aisle watching the foal through the open stall door. When the medication began to wear off, Satin again started to kick at Kezzie, so I had to give her the second shot. After many long hours, Satin accepted her role as mother, and we felt it was safe to leave the two alone while we got some much-needed sleep."

Carrie frowned. "That doesn't make sense. Why didn't Satin want her baby?"

"That's a good question. I wondered that too. I also remember thinking that as bad as it was for Satin to reject Kezzie, it was much harder to understand why some people abandon their children. In the Bible it says, 'When my father and my mother forsake me, then the Lord will take care of me.'[1] And in Deuteronomy, God promises that He will never leave us or forsake us."[2]

1 Psalm 27:10
2 Deuteronomy 31:6

Grandma got up from the picnic table and patted Kezzie's neck. "Carrie, you may never know what happened to your biological parents, but I hope someday you will come to know that God is your heavenly Father and that He loves you very much. He's already taking care of you by bringing you to the Robinson's and next door to me."

Carrie sat with her chin resting on both hands, staring at Kezzie and thinking about the story. Rosie's grandmother talked as if she knew God personally. He was supposed to be her Father? Carrie didn't know what it felt like to have a father. She supposed she had one somewhere. She didn't remember ever seeing him, but something deep inside her ached to know him. "I go to church with the Robinsons, but no one there talks about God the way you do."

"My stories might not make sense to everyone, but horses help me understand our relationship to God." Grandma put her arm around Carrie. "Trust me. He has a plan for you. It says that in the Bible. He wants to give you hope and a future."[3]

Carrie squirmed a little. She wasn't used to people hugging her. Hope and a future? She just hoped the Robinsons wouldn't decide to send her to another foster home. "Thank you, Mrs. Watson."

"Would you like to call me 'Grandma'? 'Mrs. Watson' sounds a bit formal."

"Okay, Mrs. Wats—" Carrie giggled. "I mean Grandma."

"Why don't you help Rosie take Kezzie back to her stall? I'll run over and talk to—oh dear, I've forgotten your foster mother's name."

"Judy." Carrie jumped down from the picnic table. "Judy and Ross are my new foster mom and dad."

---

3   Jeremiah 29:11

"I'll go over and talk to them about riding lessons."

Carrie watched as Rosie dismounted. "Are you mad at me?"

"I was." Rosie faced her with her arms crossed. "But it was my fault too. I shouldn't have let you get to me."

"So you're not mad at me anymore?"

"Nah." Rosie held out Kezzie's lead rope. "Do you want to lead her?"

Carrie smiled and nodded. "That was a neat story about Kezzie and Satin. Your grandma is nice."

Rosie held up her arm and pointed to her horsehair bracelet. "If you think that was interesting, wait until you hear about Jet."

9

Carrie's First Ride

꒦

Maybe God really was looking out for her. Mrs. Robinson had agreed to the riding lessons, and the late-spring sky the following day was a brilliant blue and cloudless. The temperature had inched into the seventies for the first time that year. Carrie couldn't have asked for better weather for her first ride. She stood at Kezzie's left side next to Grandma and looked up at the saddle. The horse seemed so tall. Fear suddenly gripped her, and she wasn't sure she wanted to ride after all.

Grandma apparently hadn't noticed her second thoughts. "Put your foot into the stirrup."

Carrie had to go through with it now or they would know she was afraid. She didn't want Rosie to make fun of her, so she slowly raised her right foot.

"Wrong one," Rosie laughed. "If you start with that foot, you'll end up riding backwards."

"Oh, yeah. I knew that." Carrie was a few months younger and an inch shorter than Rosie. Carrie was blond and fair-skinned with blue eyes, while Rosie was dark-haired with brown eyes. Both girls were thin and wiry, but strong for their size.

"Here let me give you a boost." Grandma laced her fingers together and held her arms out to Carrie. "Put your knee in here, and I'll help you up. Give a little hop, then grab the saddle and pull."

Carrie jumped and grabbed for the saddle. She felt herself rising rapidly as Grandma lifted her.

"Swing your leg over," Rosie yelled.

Carrie swung her right leg around and kicked Kezzie in the hindquarters. The horse flinched but otherwise didn't move. "Oops, sorry, girl."

Grandma smiled as Carrie settled into the saddle. "I'm glad you're still on. I had a girl several years ago who didn't hold on to the saddle. The first time I helped her up, she went right on over and ended up flat on the ground on the other side of the horse."

Carrie frowned and looked down at Grandma. "Wow! Kezzie is so tall."

"Not really." Rosie shook her head. "She's barely a horse."

"What do you mean?" Carrie frowned. "She looks like a horse to me."

"Kezzie is 14.3 hands[1]. If she were two inches shorter, she'd be a pony," Rosie explained. "Grandma says Scamper will be around fourteen hands when he's full grown, so he'll always be a pony."

Carrie shrugged. "I don't know what you mean by hands."

---

1   One hand equals 4" so Kezzie is 59" tall at the withers. Horses are 14.2 hands or taller. Ponies are shorter than 14.2.

"Don't worry," Rosie said. "I'll explain it later. I bet you want to get started."

Grandma took the reins and led Kezzie toward the arena.

"She's fast!" Carrie wobbled in the saddle and almost grabbed for the horn, but she was determined not to let Rosie know she was afraid.

Rosie pulled her camera from her pocket and ran backwards in front of them, snapping photos of Carrie's first ride.

Once inside the arena, Grandma pulled the reins up and hooked them over the saddle horn. "We'll begin with the basics: starting, walking, turning, and stopping. Kezzie is wearing a bridle on her head. The metal thing inside her mouth is called a bit. Attached to the bit on each side are reins. You use the reins to give Kezzie signals to stop and turn."

Carrie concentrated on Grandma's instructions. She wanted to do everything correctly.

"With a well-trained horse like Kezzie, you can give the signals lightly. Horses can feel when a tiny fly lands on them. They're very sensitive animals."

Carrie nodded. She had seen Kezzie twitch her skin to get flies off.

"Have you ever watched an old western on TV—where the riders jerk and pull on the reins?"

"Yes."

"Good," Grandma said. "That's exactly how I don't want you to ride!" She pointed to Carrie's face. "Imagine having a metal bit inside your own mouth. How do you think it would feel to have someone jerk on your reins?"

Carrie's hand flew up to cover her mouth. "Ow! That would hurt."

"Right. So remember to take it easy on Kezzie's mouth."

Carrie nodded.

"We'll start with direct reining; it's the simplest. Hold one rein in each hand like this." Grandma drew a rein up through her fist to show Carrie how it should be held.

Carrie carefully adjusted the reins in each of her hands.

"Gently pull on the right rein to go right and the left rein to turn left. To stop, say 'whoa' and pull on both reins evenly. To go, squeeze your legs against Kezzie's sides and say 'walk.'"

Carrie took a deep breath. She had a tingly feeling in her stomach. The fear was gradually turning into excitement. "I think I'm ready."

"Kezzie is a patient teacher. You'll make some mistakes at first, but she'll forgive you as long as you're not mean to her." Grandma pointed to her left. "Let's see you walk in a circle."

"Walk." Carrie squeezed her legs, and Kezzie started off with the long, rolling walk of a gaited horse.

When Carrie pulled the left rein, Kezzie turned in a small, tight circle, walked straight back to Grandma, and stopped. "Hey, Kezzie." Carrie frowned. "I didn't tell you to do that." She looked to Grandma for help. "Why did she go back to you?"

"You're oversteering. Pull easier next time, and as soon as you feel her start to turn, stop pulling." Grandma demonstrated with a set of invisible reins. "She'll come back to me every time if you give her half a chance. She's a bit spoiled."

Carrie tried again, and this time Kezzie made a bigger circle.

"Much better." Grandma nodded. "You have naturally soft hands. With more practice, you'll figure it out. It's mostly a matter of feel."

Carrie was smiling so broadly that her mouth was beginning to hurt, but she couldn't stop. She was riding! Grandma had said she had soft hands. She wasn't sure what that meant, but it sounded like a good thing. She reached down to pat Kezzie's shoulder. "Good girl, Kezzie! Good girl."

Rosie climbed the fence and leaned toward her grandmother. "I'm going to ask Mom if Carrie can spend the night."

"That's a good idea," Grandma said. "Are you sad that you have to share Kezzie now?"

"No. I think it will be even more fun. Besides, Scamper is my horse. How much longer will it be before I can start riding him?"

Grandma kept her eyes on Carrie and Kezzie. When she didn't answer, Rosie thought she hadn't heard the question. She was about to repeat it when Grandma finally replied.

"Considering your size and how stocky Scamper is, I'd say you'll be able to start riding him lightly when he's two."[2]

"That's almost two whole years from now," Rosie moaned. "That will take forever."

"Yes, you'll be eleven then, practically an old lady," Grandma teased. "When you get to be my age, two years goes by much faster. We'll continue your lessons on Kezzie, and you can help with Scamper's groundwork. Then when the time comes, you'll both be ready."

---

2   See the Horse Safety notes at the end of the book.

Rosie couldn't wait. Two years sounded like an eternity to her, but it would be fun to help Grandma train Scamper. She turned back to watch Carrie on Kezzie. Could she and this girl become friends?

10

The Missing Helmet

꒦

Scamper and Kezzie stood tied to the wash rack beside the barn. The girls had bathed them, and they were drying under the warm spring sun. Scamper, now a strong, stocky two-year-old, stood about fourteen hands tall just as Grandma had predicted.

Carrie sprayed detangler on Kezzie's tail and pulled a comb through it.

Grandma coiled the hose and set it to the side of the wash rack. "You girls are like two peas in a pod. I rarely see one of you without the other anymore."

Carrie looked at Rosie and giggled. "Remember when we first met and I got you in trouble—when I dared you to get on Kezzie?"

"I was so mad at you," Rosie said. "You weren't very nice then."

"I know." Carrie nodded. "I'm glad you decided to be my friend anyway. I never had a best friend before."

Grandma smiled. "Now I have two wonderful assistants to help me with all the work around here. By the way, have you cleaned the stalls yet?"

"We finished those a long time ago," Rosie replied.

"Okay then, I guess it's time."

"Time for what?" Rosie asked.

"Your first ride on Scamper!" Grandma beamed. "The day you've been waiting on for two years is finally here! I can't wait to see you ride him."

Rosie stood as if frozen and smiled briefly. "Are you sure he's strong enough to hold me?"

"Strong enough?" Grandma patted Scamper's shoulder. "This boy is built like a tank. As light as you are, he'll be fine. Carrie can help me saddle him while you grab your helmet."

Rosie started slowly toward the tack room while Grandma led Scamper into the barn. She was excited about riding her pony for the first time, but fears nagged at her. What if he bucked—or ran away with her? Scamper had carried a saddle many times but never a rider.

She opened the tack room door, halfheartedly looked around, then closed it again and stood in the aisle for a few minutes.

"Rosie?"

She could hear her grandmother calling her. Rosie walked down the barn aisle—empty-handed.

Grandma held the bridle up and straightened the straps. "Where's your helmet?"

"I … I … uh," Rosie stammered. "I … couldn't find it."

Grandma studied her. "What do you mean you couldn't find it? It's always hanging right there in the tack room when you're not using it."

Carrie looked back and forth from Grandma to Rosie.

Rosie stared at the ground. "I didn't see it in there," she said softly.

Grandma was quiet for a moment. "Hmm. *The Case of the Missing Helmet* reminds me of *The Case of the Missing Swimming Suit*."

Rosie and Carrie both seemed perplexed by that statement and waited for Grandma's explanation.

Grandma hooked the bridle over the horn of Scamper's saddle. "It was about thirty years ago. My oldest daughter, Lisa, was nine. She was taking swimming lessons and had finished the first course. We were getting ready for the lessons the morning she was to advance to the second level."

Rosie took a deep breath and leaned back against the barn wall. She didn't know how Grandma did it, but she had a feeling her grandmother knew exactly what was going on with the helmet.

"It was almost time to leave, and I hadn't seen Lisa for a while. I called upstairs to see whether she was ready to go. After a long silence, I heard her say, 'I can't find my swimming suit, Mom,' in a tone nearly identical to the one you just used."

Rosie fiddled with the end of her braid and avoided eye contact.

"I was puzzled, because I remembered washing the swimming suit after the last lesson and putting it in her dresser. When I went upstairs, that's exactly where it was. Do you have any idea why Lisa said she couldn't find her swimming suit?"

Grandma looked at Carrie who shrugged and shook her head. Then she turned to Rosie.

How did her grandmother always seem to know what she was feeling? Rosie hesitated. "Was she afraid, Grandma?"

"Yes. She *was* afraid. I didn't realize it at first, but later Lisa told me that in the next swim class, the kids had to dive in off the side of the pool, and she was afraid to try that. Could something like that be the problem with the missing helmet?"

Rosie leaned against Scamper. "Grandma, I'm so used to riding Kezzie now. I sort of panicked at the thought of riding Scamper for the first time. What if he bucks me off?"

Grandma wrapped her arm around Rosie. "Did you think I was going to turn you loose on him? Like all his other training, we'll do things gradually. First, all I want you to do is get on him, sit for a few minutes, and then get off. I'll hold him the whole time. Can you do that?"

Rosie smiled and nodded. She faced Scamper and raised her foot toward the stirrup.

Grandma tapped her on the shoulder. "Aren't you forgetting something?"

"Oh!" Rosie patted her head. "My helmet!" She trotted off toward the tack room.

"Grab Carrie's while you're in there," Grandma called.

Rosie reappeared moments later—helmets in hand. She tossed one to Carrie and buckled her own on her head. Within seconds, she was on Scamper's back. He turned, sniffed her pant leg, and looked up at Rosie as if to ask what she was doing on his back, but he stood calmly.

"Yay, you did it!" Carrie cheered.

70

Rosie leaned forward, put her arms around Scamper's neck, and hugged him tightly.

"I was sure he would be fine," Grandma said. "Otherwise I wouldn't have asked you to get on him. I should have explained everything so you would have been more prepared."

"It's all right. I can't believe I'm finally riding Scamper."

"Hop down," Grandma instructed. "We need to repeat that over and over until he gets used to it."

Rosie glanced at Carrie. "Let's take turns."

Scamper stood patiently as the girls mounted and dismounted.

After they practiced that a dozen times, Scamper seemed completely comfortable with the process.

"Let's move out to the arena now," Grandma suggested.

Rosie smiled broadly as Grandma led her to the arena. "I still can't believe I'm riding my own horse. It feels so different from riding Kezzie. He's wider with a shorter but faster stride."

Grandma lengthened the lead line. "I'll lunge him in small circles so you can begin teaching him to respond to the bit."

Rosie and Carrie took turns working with Scamper on turning, stopping, and starting. Grandma was impressed with both the girls' and Scamper's performance. "That's a good day's work," she announced after about thirty minutes.

All three of them praised the pony enthusiastically as they unsaddled and brushed him. Scamper seemed to understand what an important day it was. He held his head high, looking as proud as if he had just won the Kentucky Derby.

"Aren't you glad you gave it a try?" Grandma asked.

"Yeah. I'm kind of embarrassed," Rosie said. "It was ridiculous to be afraid."

"You should have let me go first," Carrie teased. "I wouldn't have been scared."

"Right." Rosie rolled her eyes. "Because you've trained so many horses."

Carrie smiled and resumed brushing Scamper.

Grandma leaned against the stall and watched the girls. "When I was a teen, I had a scary experience with my horse."

Rosie paused and looked over at her grandmother.

"After a recent rain, the ground was wet. I was cantering in an arena when the horse suddenly slipped in a muddy spot and fell. She went down on her side, right on top of my leg."

"Ouch!" Carrie bent her leg at the knee and held it for a moment.

"Fortunately I was only bruised and sore, not seriously injured."

"Were you scared then, Grandma?" Rosie asked.

"Yes. And to be honest, it still makes me a bit afraid sometimes. I never liked to ride too fast after that. I guess the idea that the horse might fall on me again is always lurking in the back of my mind. But imagine how much I would have missed out on if I had let that fear keep me from ever riding again."

"If you hadn't kept riding, Mom probably wouldn't have ridden, and I might not have learned how to ride either," Rosie said.

"And then, I never would have been able to ride," Carrie added.

Grandma continued. "The Bible says that God has not given us a spirit of fear, but of power and of love and of a sound mind.[1] That would be a good verse for both of you to memorize. Of course, sometimes it makes sense to have some fear—you wouldn't want to jump on Scamper today and ride him down the road. He's not ready for that yet."

Rosie nodded.

"Fear is wrong when it keeps us from doing something God wants us to do. We need to trust God and obey, and He will help us overcome our fears."

Rosie tossed her brush into the tack bucket. "I love to ride fast."

Grandma laughed. "You're like your Aunt Julie. She was two years old the first time she rode. I had her on the saddle in front of me. We walked around for a while, then I trotted a bit.

---

1   2 Timothy 1:7 NKJV

I was worried she might be afraid, on a big horse for the first time, so I stopped, leaned forward, and asked her how she was doing. I still remember the grin on her face when she said, 'Go faster, Mommy!'"

Grandma smiled and watched the girls finish grooming Scamper. After they turned him out with Kezzie in the pasture, the three walked down the path toward the house, one girl on each side of Grandma.

"Scamper needs to be ridden as often as possible now, so whenever either of you can help me, we'll continue his training."

"School will be out soon, then I can come over every day," Carrie offered. "Mrs. Judy hasn't been feeling well. I have to be quiet when she's resting."

"Oh?" Grandma frowned. "I'm sorry to hear she's not well. I'll stop over to see if there's anything I can do for her."

Rosie made a face at her friend. "You used to be jealous of me because I'm homeschooled. Now I'm jealous of you because you live next door to Grandma and can come over whenever you want. I only get to come a few times a week."

Grandma smiled. "I think you'll like this idea, Rosie."

"What idea?"

"Your mom, your aunts, and I were talking, and we've decided to have something we're calling Cousins Camp."

"Cousins Camp?" Rosie looked at her grandmother. "What's that?"

"Exactly what it sounds like. All your cousins, aunts, and uncles are coming to spend a week here at my house for our own summer camp. And, of course, Carrie is included too."

"Wow, Cousins Camp sounds like fun!" Rosie said. "You'll love my cousins, Carrie. I haven't seen Lauren for about a year. She lives in Texas with my Aunt Lisa and Uncle Robert."

"Julie's bringing four of her horses so no one will have to share," Grandma said. "That way you'll all get plenty of riding time."

"Is Cousins Camp next week?" Carrie asked.

"No," Grandma laughed. "Not for several months. That will give us time to get Scamper ready."

"I can't wait!" Rosie exclaimed. "I have an important question for Aunt Lisa when she gets here."

"Oh, what's that?" Grandma asked.

Rosie had already started to run ahead on the path. She stopped and turned around. "I'm going to ask her if she ever found her swimming suit."

11

Camp Preparations

Rosie coughed and waved her hand in front of her face to keep from breathing the dust Kezzie and Scamper were kicking up in the arena. The girls and Grandma had worked with Scamper nearly every day over the past few months, and he had proven to be a fast learner. Rosie spotted her grandmother walking their direction, and she urged Scamper toward the gate.

"Oh! This helmet is driving me crazy! It's *so* hot and itchy." Rosie bent her head down, stretched the sleeve of her T-shirt, and used it to wipe the sweat that dripped steadily down her face. She stuck two fingers inside the helmet as far as they would go, but she couldn't reach the itchy spot. "Grandma, can I take this thing off for a minute?"

"No! You know the rules. If you're on a horse, that helmet stays on your head." Grandma held out two glasses of icy lemonade. "It's dry as a bone out here. I can't remember when it rained last."

The girls drained the drinks.

"Ahhh—that hit the spot! Thank you." Carrie wiped her mouth on her arm and handed the glass back.

"Walk the horses awhile, and then hose them off. Rosie, I'm impressed with the progress you've made. You sure know how to communicate with that pony. Maybe you'll be a horse trainer like your Aunt Julie when you grow up."

Rosie smiled and patted Scamper's neck. She would love to be a horse trainer. Did Grandma really mean it? Or was she just being nice?

Grandma opened the gate, and the girls rode the horses out of the arena.

"I can't believe everyone will be here tomorrow for Cousins Camp. I hope your cousins will like me." Carrie patted Kezzie's sweaty neck. "Oh, yuck. You need a bath, girl."

"I'm sure you'll have a great time with everyone," Rosie said.

Carrie didn't look so sure. "I've met all of them when they visited Grandma—except Lauren, but I don't really know them."

"It will be fine. You'll see." Rosie couldn't understand why Carrie was so worried about her cousins.

Grandma had taught the girls to always cool the horses down before putting them up after a ride. That had been a challenge lately with the August temperatures hovering in the nineties.

"Let's take them to the woods," Rosie suggested. "It will be a little cooler there." They rode to the woods and walked around the trail a few times. When the horses were as cool as possible, the girls returned to the barn.

They tied Scamper and Kezzie to the wash rack and unsaddled them. Rosie turned on the water and aimed the hose at Scamper. The dirt on his coat dissolved into mud and combined with his foamy sweat to form chocolatey rivers that ran down his side and dripped onto the concrete. Scamper seemed to enjoy the cool shower. When Rosie brought the hose around to wash his head, he grabbed it between his teeth and yanked it from her hands.

"Hey, give that back, you silly boy!" Rosie tugged on the hose, but instead of letting go, Scamper pulled harder, like a dog playing tug-of-war. He bobbed his head up and down a few times, splashing water all over her, then he lost interest and dropped the hose.

Rosie picked it up and handed it to Carrie. "Here. You can use this now." She watched as her friend sprayed Kezzie. "When Grandma was a girl, she took her pony, Dolly, to the fair and let her drink lemonade from a cup. She shared her fair fries with her too."

Carrie smiled. "I've never heard of a pony eating french fries. I hate fair fries—too greasy!"

Rosie shrugged. "Dolly loved them. I love fair food too."

"That's not surprising. You love all food!" Carrie moved to the other side of Kezzie. "Are you excited about taking Scamper to the fair?"

"Yeah. I can't wait!" Rosie twirled the lead rope around while she waited for Carrie to finish. Suddenly she stopped. "Hey, I have an idea. You should take Kezzie!"

Carrie's face lit up. "To the fair? Do you think Grandma would let me?"

"Let's ask her after we put the horses up." Why hadn't she thought of that before? It would be much more fun if Carrie could go to the fair with her. Rosie thought about the best way to convince her grandmother.

When Carrie finished, the girls led the horses through the gate into the field and turned them loose. Kezzie made a beeline for the dustiest spot in the pasture, circled around twice, and dropped to the ground.

"Ew! I was afraid she would do that," Carrie moaned. "You crazy horse! Do you know how hard I worked to get you clean?"

Kezzie rolled over once, made a funny groaning noise, and then rolled over again.

Rosie climbed on the wooden fence for a better view. "Once more, Kezzie," she called. "Grandma told me when she was young they used to say a horse was worth a hundred dollars for each time it rolled completely over. I say it's one thousand now."

The girls both watched Kezzie, waiting to see whether she would increase her value. She was still for a few minutes, then rolled over one last time.

"Yay!" Carrie cheered. "You're worth three thousand dollars, Kezzie!"

Scamper stood nearby watching Kezzie. Apparently he thought a nice roll sounded like a great idea.[1] Soon he was down on the ground too.

"That fat old boy won't make it over once," Carrie laughed.

"My horse is not fat—or old!" Why was she always making fun of Scamper? As Carrie stood at the fence, Rosie quietly climbed down, grabbed the hose, and blasted her in the middle of the back with a stream of water.

---

1   allelomimetic behavior - If you want to impress your parents or friends, casually throw this word into the conversation. It's a combination of the word *mimic* and the genetic term *allele* and indicates behavior that is copied by another animal.

"Aagh, that's cold!" Carrie lunged at Rosie and tried to yank the hose away from her.

When Rosie spun around to keep the hose from Carrie, she spotted her grandmother coming out of the barn. "Oops!"

Grandma stopped, put both hands on her hips, and stared at them for a moment.

Rosie dropped the hose and grinned sheepishly. "Um. Carrie had a dirty spot on her back, and I was helping her clean it off."

"Uh-huh." Grandma walked over and turned the water off. "Why don't you two put that energy into something productive—like helping me get ready for Cousins Camp?"

"Sure, Grandma." Rosie coiled the hose and dropped it beside the wash rack. "What do you want us to do?"

"We'll use your mom's old room for the girls' bunkhouse. You can arrange the makeshift beds for the five of you and put up some of the decorations I bought. Jared will have Julie's room to himself."

"What are your cousins' names again?" Carrie asked.

"Everyone in Julie's family starts with 'J,' that makes it easy to remember. Jared is eleven, same as you and me. The twins are Jessie and Jamie. They're eight."

"How do you tell them apart?"

"You can't by looking at them. They're identical. You'll learn to tell who is who by the way they act. If one of them is stirring up trouble, you'll know it's Jessie. Jamie's quieter."

"Okay."

"Aunt Lisa only has Lauren. She's twelve, the oldest of all the cousins."

81

"Jared, Jessie, Jamie, Lauren. Jared, Jessie, Jamie, Lauren." Carrie chanted in time with her steps as they all made their way to the house.

"Carrie and I have a question for you." Rosie figured it would be harder for her grandmother to say "No" to Carrie, but she knew Carrie wouldn't ask for herself.

Grandma fanned her damp face with her hand. "Let's get inside first—in the air conditioning."

Rosie sprinted ahead and opened the back door. They hurried inside, and she darted toward the couch.

"Oh no you don't!" Grandma stopped her almost in midair. "You're not sitting on my furniture with those wet, dirty clothes."

Rosie stood up straight and felt a sudden chill as the air conditioning hit her wet shirt. "Grandma, we were wondering if Carrie could take Kezzie to the fair."

"Hmm." Grandma looked from Rosie to Carrie. "That sounds like a good idea. Kezzie would be lonely here by herself with Scamper gone. I'll need to discuss it with Judy and Ross first though."

Rosie grinned at Carrie. The fair would be so much fun with her friend and both their horses there.

"We'll think about that when Cousins Camp is over." Grandma pointed toward the stairs. "Put some dry clothes on, then you can get the bedrooms ready for our guests."

That was as good as a yes to the girls. They ran for the stairs, chattering excitedly about their plans for the fair.

Rosie put her hand to her forehead to shield her eyes from the early morning sun as she glanced out the hayloft door. She could see as far as the Robinsons' house to the right. Beyond that, the narrow country road curved and disappeared from view. She didn't see any sign of an approaching vehicle—only a few cows in the field across the road. She moo'ed to them, but they didn't even look up from their grazing.

"When will they get here?" Carrie asked for the tenth time.

The girls had stationed themselves as lookouts in the hayloft nearly an hour before. They wanted to be the first to see the cousins arrive. Jemimah and Katy, the barn cats, were watching also; waiting patiently for an unsuspecting mouse to emerge from one of the tunnels between the bales of hay.

Carrie leaned back against the barn wall. "You know, for the longest time I thought Grandma's sign said 'Sunrise Stable.' It was only recently that I noticed it had an 'o' instead of a 'u.' She spelled it 'Son' on purpose, right? It's about God's Son rising from the dead?"

"Yeah. You know Grandma. When people tell her she spelled the name wrong, that gives her a chance to tell them about Jesus."

Rosie peeked out the door again. "Aunt Julie's here!" She ran for the ladder, nearly tripping over Carrie.

They both scrambled down from the loft and stood in front of the barn, watching Julie's truck and trailer roll slowly down the lane.

12

Cousins

⚘

When Julie's truck stopped, Jared was the first one out, followed by his twin sisters, Jessie and Jamie. Rosie wished her cousins could visit more often, but they lived an hour away, and Julie was busy with homeschooling and her horse-training business.

Rosie's mother and Julie looked enough alike to be twins. In fact, Rosie thought her mom, and her aunts: Julie and Lisa could easily pass for triplets. She loved it when the whole family got together and the three of them talked about the things they used to do when they were kids. She wished she had a brother or sister, but at least she had a best friend now, and she was going to spend an entire week with her cousins and Carrie.

Julie stretched and walked over to the girls. "Hey, Rosie, how are you? And this must be Carrie. I think we've met before, but it's been a while. You girls ready for a fun week?"

Carrie smiled and nodded, but she suddenly seemed to have lost the ability to speak.

"I could hardly sleep last night." Rosie stared at Carrie. Why was she acting so shy all of a sudden?

"Carrie, this is Jessie." Julie put her hand on one of the girls' shoulders. "And this is Jamie." The twins' shoulder-length brown hair was cut in the same style and pulled back in short pony tails. They were dressed identically, in blue jeans, pink T-shirts, and brown cowboy boots.

"And," Julie motioned toward her son, "you probably figured out this is Jared."

"Hi, Carrie." Jared nodded. Although the same age as Rosie and Carrie, he was four inches taller and looked older. When they were younger, Jared had always teased Rosie that, "taller means older," when in reality Rosie was a few weeks older than her only boy cousin.

Carrie smiled and nodded back.

Jessie and Jamie ran toward their grandmother, who was coming out of the barn.

Jared grabbed a lead rope and walked toward the trailer. "Where do you want the horses, Mom?"

"Put them out in the arena for now, Jared," Grandma directed. "Kezzie and Scamper are in the barn. They'll all have a chance to get acquainted later."

Rosie introduced each of the horses to Carrie as Jared and Julie unloaded them from the trailer. First were two Paints that belonged to Jessie and Jamie. The girls' horses were also sisters. Jessie's was a six-year-old, brown-and-white Paint named Patches. Jamie's horse, Pearl, was two years older and black-and-white. The twins had begun competing in youth barrel racing that summer. Sometimes Jessie came out ahead; other times it was Jamie.

Next off the trailer was Jared's tall, rangy buckskin, Scout. Jared used the gelding for barrels, pole bending, and reining. Rosie was a little envious. Julie's kids had all begun riding practically as soon as they could walk. All three were already competing in events that Rosie hadn't even tried.

"Wait until you see the next horse." Rosie pointed as Julie backed her 16.3 hand bay Thoroughbred mare, Elektra, out of the trailer. "Isn't she the biggest horse you've ever seen?"

Carrie's eyes widened. "She's huge! I remember when I thought Kezzie was tall."

"Julie jumps Elektra," Rosie explained. "But she's so gentle, nearly anyone can ride her. You can ride her western or english."

As Rosie ran to open the gate to the arena, she spotted a compact car turning in to the drive. "There's Aunt Lisa!"

Lisa stopped her car and spoke through the rolled-down window. "Sorry, our plane was late. Then I dropped Robert off at Kristy's house, but we finally made it!"

Lauren ran to join her cousins. Although taller than Rosie, she was not as tall as Jared. She had long blond hair and her father's deep blue eyes.

After everyone had a chance to greet Lisa and Lauren, Grandma whistled loudly to get their attention. "You've probably been wondering what you'll be doing this week."

Rosie felt as if she might burst with excitement. She didn't know what activities had been planned, but as long as it involved horses, it would be fun.

"It might not be quite what you expected," Grandma paused until everyone focused on her. "We have three hundred bales of hay to stack, a barn to paint, and fences to repair."

Rosie raised her eyebrows and looked at Carrie, who shrugged her shoulders. Grandma was right. This was not what she had expected for Cousins Camp. *Was this one of her grandmother's jokes?* "You're kidding—aren't you?"

"Kind of," Grandma laughed. "Don't look so gloomy. Your dads will do most of the hard work. We'll help them each day, but there will still be plenty of time for riding. And—on Thursday, we're leaving for a two-day campout and trail ride at a state park—aunts, uncles, cousins, everyone!"

A big smile spread across Rosie's face. Cousins Camp was beginning to sound like fun again.

Grandma pointed to the backpacks and suitcases scattered over the ground in front of the barn. "Let's get this stuff put away; then you can ride."

Rosie led the way into the house and up to the girls' room. She and Carrie had done their best to make the room look like a ranch bunkhouse. One of the bunk bed posts held a coiled lariat. A straw cowboy hat had been placed on the other. A wrinkled pair of worn leather boots stood guard by the door, an old saddle rested on a rack in the corner, and a steer skull, complete with long, curved horns sat on top of the dresser.

"Jessie and Jamie, because you're the youngest, Carrie and I decided to let you have first choice on the beds."

Jessie ran past the bunks to the back of the room and jumped on an air mattress. "Why do you always have to say we're the youngest?"

"Sorry." Rosie made a face at her cousin. "But you two *are* the youngest." She turned to Lauren. "You and Carrie can have the bunk beds. I'll take the cot next to the twins."

"I wanted to be next to you, Carrie," Jamie said.

Rosie could tell from Carrie's expression that she didn't know which twin was talking to her. No one except family could tell Jessie and Jamie apart. If they weren't speaking or doing something, even Rosie had a hard time telling who was who.

Carrie smiled and tossed her things on the top bunk. "Jessie?"

"Nope, I'm Jamie."

"No, she's not!" Jessie leaped up from the air mattress. "She's trying to trick you. I'm Jamie!"

Oh, brother. Rosie clapped her hand onto the top of her head. Jessie was stirring up trouble already. She pointed to the girl beside Carrie. "That's Jamie. And that—" She pointed to the other twin as she ran out of the room, "was Jessie."

"I'm sorry," Carrie said. "I'll try not to get you mixed up again."

"It's okay," Jamie said. "It happens a lot. We're used to it."

Rosie picked up a box from the dresser and showed it to the others. "Mom got this game for us—Horse-opoly. Tonight we can all play it before we go to bed."

"I've played that before," Lauren said. "It's fun, but it takes a long time."

When everyone was back at the barn, Grandma sat on the tack box with the kids gathered around her. "This week, you'll each ride a different horse than the one you're used to. It will be good experience for you. And, because Lauren doesn't have a horse of her own—"

"Yet!" Lauren interrupted.

"Right." Grandma smiled at her. "Yet. I'm putting you on Kezzie. She won't give you any trouble. Rosie, you'll ride Elektra."

Rosie's eyes widened. She had ridden Aunt Julie's horse once before, but only a few times around the ring.

"Carrie will ride Pearl," Grandma continued. "Jared, you take Scamper. That leaves Scout for Jessie and Patches for Jamie."

Rosie whispered to Jared, "Take good care of my horse."

Jared rolled his eyes. "Do you think I don't know how to ride? I've been riding for longer than you have."

"He's special," Rosie said. "Be nice to him."

"Don't worry. I'll be careful with your little baby."

"Don't let him hear you say he's little. He thinks he's a big horse." Rosie wasn't worried. Jared could have a bit of an attitude at times, but he was a good rider and loved animals.

As Grandma finished the assignments, Kristy walked into the barn. "The guys are on their way to pick up the hay. They didn't want my help, so here I am. What are you all sitting around for? Let's get started!" She clapped her hands, and the kids leaped into action.

Julie, Kristy, and Lisa helped them groom, saddle, and bridle the horses. When Julie finished saddling Elektra, Rosie stared at the stirrup. "There's no way I can get on this horse by myself."

"Don't worry. I can't get on her either, without a mounting block," Julie said. "Here, I'll give you a boost."

When she was mounted, Rosie felt as if she towered over all the other horses and riders. "Elektra is so tall!" She remembered how, not that long ago, she had been afraid to ride Scamper for the first time. The months she had spent helping her grandmother train the pony had made her a more confident rider. Elektra was much taller than Scamper, but the mare's height didn't bother her. It would be fun riding Julie's horse for the week.

Everyone met in the arena. Kezzie and Scamper seemed surprised to be sharing their territory with the newcomers. The adults stationed themselves so they could keep an eye on everyone and give a few pointers here and there.

They rode around the arena until everyone seemed comfortable, then Grandma called them into the middle. "We're going to have a contest. Some of you have done this before. It's called the egg and spoon race. Lisa will give each of you a spoon, then Kristy and Julie will pass out the eggs. Place your egg on the spoon. You must hold the spoon near the end of the handle. Hold the reins in your other hand. I'll tell you when to walk, trot, and canter. As soon as you drop your egg, you're out, and you have to stand in the center of the arena. The last one with an egg wins."

Rosie had been in egg and spoon contests before, but she had never won one. She looked around at the others, then patted Elektra's neck. "Let's win this. Okay, girl?"

13
Eggs and Hay

After Grandma finished giving the egg and spoon instructions, Jared slouched back on Scamper, looking as if he were bored with the whole thing. "What do I get when I win?"

"When *you* win?" Rosie stared at him. Why did he assume he would be the winner? That only made her more determined to beat him.

"Your name will be recorded in the Cousins Camp Hall of Fame as the first egg and spoon champion," Grandma said.

"Oh wow! What an honor!" Jared took an egg from Lisa. "What about some prize money?"

Grandma walked over to Carrie.

Rosie wondered whether her grandmother had heard Jared. Maybe she was just ignoring his question. She held out her spoon, and Lisa set an egg on it. Rosie placed her thumb over the egg to keep it from falling off before they even got started. She didn't care what the prize was; she just wanted to beat Jared.

"Everyone walk," Grandma called out.

As they began walking, Rosie stared at her egg as if watching it intently would keep it on the spoon.

After several laps with all the eggs intact, Grandma asked them to trot.

Almost immediately, Lauren's egg hit the ground, and she walked Kezzie toward the center of the ring.

"That's okay," Grandma encouraged her. "You'll do better next time."

Rosie listened for her grandmother to call out the next gait. This was easy so far.

"Canter."

94

Splat! Rosie saw Carrie's egg fall to the ground when she tried to get Pearl into a canter.

Carrie rode to the center and stopped beside Lauren. It looked like Jamie was also having difficulty. Her egg took a dive soon after Carrie's.

Rosie looked around, then whispered to Elektra, "Just a little bit longer. Only two more to beat." Jessie would probably be the next one out, then it would be between her and Jared.

"Whoa!" Grandma yelled.

Scamper had been trained to respond to Grandma's voice commands. Rosie smiled as she watched her pony slide to a stop ahead of her. The sudden stop caused Jared's egg to sail over Scamper's head and splatter on the ground.

Rosie steadied her egg hand and pulled gently on Elektra's reins. "What happened, Jared? I thought you were going to win."

Jared frowned. "That's not fair! Scamper stopped before I told him to."

Grandma waved away his protests.

Jared turned and stuck his tongue out at Rosie, then joined the girls in the middle.

Rosie couldn't believe Jared was out. Jessie was her only competition now. It shouldn't be hard to beat her. Rosie pictured her name in the Cousins Camp Hall of Fame—wherever that was going to be.

"Trot," Grandma called.

Elektra was usually ridden English at a faster trot than Rosie was accustomed to. They passed Jessie and Scout. The big gelding barely picked up his feet. His gait wasn't much faster than a walk, and Jessie didn't seem to move in the saddle.

Rosie frowned and stood in her stirrups to keep herself from bouncing so much. "Easy, girl. Slow down. It's not that kind of a race."

Bounce, bounce, bounce... Her egg wobbled with the rhythm of Elektra's trot.

"Reverse at a trot," Grandma said.

"Easy. Slow down, girl." Rosie signaled the mare to turn, but Elektra refused. Instead, the horse began trotting faster. Rosie's egg took a giant bounce. She tried to catch it with her spoon, but the egg fell to the ground.

"Oh no!" Rosie tossed her spoon into the air. She couldn't believe she'd lost to her younger cousin. Jessie would probably never let her forget it. Nevertheless, she had won fair and square. "Good job, Jess! Let's have a rematch sometime, just you and me—only on our own horses."

Jessie grinned and nodded. "I'll beat you again! Patches is even smoother than Scout."

"We'll see," Rosie said.

"What's next, Grandma?" Lauren asked.

Grandma pointed to three trucks and hay wagons ready to pull in the drive. "The hay is here!" She opened the gate. "Everybody off. Let's put the horses up, so we can help the guys with the hay."

Rosie followed the twins out of the arena. Jessie had her unbroken egg in her left hand and Scout's reins in her right as they led the horses toward the barn. Before Rosie realized what Jessie was doing, the girl had fired the egg at the person in front of her.

"Ow! What was that?" Carrie clapped her hand onto the back of her head. Sticky goo oozed through her fingers. "Ew, yuck!"

Rosie and Elektra trotted until they caught up to Carrie.

When Carrie whirled around to see who had thrown the egg at her, Jessie doubled over with laughter.

"Why did you do that?" Carrie looked as if she might cry.

Jessie laughed and shrugged.

"Jessie, that wasn't funny!" Rosie looked around. The adults were nearly at the barn. She thought about telling her mom or grandmother, but decided it wasn't worth causing a big fuss and spoiling the first day of Cousins Camp.

Jessie led Scout past them, still laughing.

"I shouldn't have come. Maybe Jessie wants it to be only the real cousins." Carrie stared at the ground.

Rosie shook her head. "No. That's just the way she is. Didn't I warn you about her? She likes to play jokes on people."

"If you're sure. I mean, I don't have to come tomorrow if she doesn't want me here."

"I'm sure it didn't have anything to do with that." Rosie put her arm around Carrie's shoulder. "Cousins Camp wouldn't be the same without you. After we take care of the horses, I'll rinse the egg out with the hose—although I think egg is supposed to be good for your hair."

"I'd rather stick to shampoo." Carrie stared at the gooey mess on her hand, then wiped it off on her jeans.

After the horses were all unsaddled, the kids led them to the pasture and turned them out. They squealed and ran around the field as they became acquainted with each other, but soon they were all grazing calmly together.

Rosie made her way to the wash rack and flipped a bucket upside down. She waved to her friend. "Carrie! Come here."

Carrie and Lauren came running. Lauren looked at the hose Rosie held. "What are you doing?"

"I'm going to rinse that mess out of Carrie's hair." Rosie motioned theatrically toward the bucket. "Welcome to my beauty parlor."

Carrie sat on the overturned bucket and wrapped her arms around her knees.

Rosie stood behind her. "Lean back toward me." She waved her hand backward. "A little more."

"If I lean any more, I'll fall over."

Laughing, Lauren grabbed Carrie's hands to keep her from tipping over.

Rosie raised the hose to the back of Carrie's head and began to rinse out the egg. "Ew. This is so gross!"

Grandma started to walk past them, then stopped and stared. "It's certainly a strange time to wash your hair. What in the world are you girls doing?"

"I… Uh…" Carrie tried to explain. "I accidentally got some… um… egg in my hair."

Grandma shook her head. "I'm not sure I want to know." She faced Rosie. "That better be all you're using that hose for, young lady."

"Who, me?" Rosie looked up innocently. "What makes you think I would do anything else with it?"

"Just a suspicion. This isn't a good time for a water fight. I need you girls on the hay wagon."

"Okay, Grandma." Rosie finished rinsing Carrie's hair, dropped the hose, and ran to turn it off.

The three girls hurried to the first hay wagon, and Rosie scrambled quickly to the top.

Lauren raised her hand to shield her eyes from the sun and glanced up at her. "How'd you do that?"

"Easy." Rosie pointed to a brace at the back of the wagon. "Hang on to that bar and pull yourself up, then climb up the bales. When you get close enough, I'll grab your arm and help you the rest of the way."

Soon all three girls were up.

Lauren reached down to pet a calico cat that was prowling around on top of the hay. "What are you doing up here?"

"That's Jemimah," Carrie explained. "She and her sister, Katy, love it when we get hay."

Rosie nodded. "That's how Grandma got them. They were tiny kittens that came in a load of hay she bought a few years ago."

"What happened to their mother?" Lauren asked.

Rosie shrugged. "I don't know. Grandma said she must have been wild. They never found her. The kittens were so small. They barely had their eyes open. I helped Grandma bottle-feed them."

Rosie sat down and scratched the top of the cat's head. "Every time we get a new load of hay, Jemimah and Katy search the wagon to see if their mother has come back for them."

"Aww, that's depressing." Lauren frowned. "Why did you have to tell me that story?"

"Are you girls going to stand there gabbing all day?" Jared yelled. "Or are you going to start tossing hay bales down?"

Rosie looked at her cousin. Was he planning to be this bossy all week? They hadn't been talking that long. Had they?

"Get down, Jemimah, before you get hurt." Carrie gently shooed the cat down the back of the wagon, and the girls began pushing bales over the side.

"Careful." Rosie held her arm out toward Carrie and Lauren. "Don't get too close to the edge."

As the girls unloaded the wagon, Jared and the adults carried the bales into the barn and stacked them.

Since the bales weighed nearly as much as the twins, and their parents wouldn't allow them on top of the wagon, they had gone to wade in the creek while everyone else worked. Rosie could hear them yelling to each other.

After filling the hay storage area in the lower part of the barn, Julie's husband, Jonathan, hooked his tractor up to an elevator they used to send the rest of the bales up to the hayloft.

There were so many people helping, that Grandma didn't have to carry any bales herself. She bustled around, passing out water bottles and encouragement.

When they were almost finished, Jonathan, peeked out the hayloft door. "Are you girls about to the bottom of that wagon? It must be 120 degrees up here."

Rosie laughed loudly when she saw her uncle. His sweaty face and arms were coated with so much dust and bits of hay that she barely recognized him. A few minutes later, her dad, her uncle Robert, and Jared came to the door for a breath of fresh air. They all looked just as grimy as Jonathan.

"Rosie will show you where the hose is so you can clean up," Grandma said. "I'll go throw some hamburgers on the grill. I'm sure you've all worked up an appetite."

The hose? Rosie grinned. Maybe she could start a water fight after all!

14
Barn Campout

Rosie licked her lips, savoring the last bite of buttery, salty corn on the cob. After everyone had eaten their fill of the grilled corn, hamburgers, and homemade potato salad, Rosie approached her grandmother. "All of us kids thought it would be fun to camp out in the barn tonight. Can we?"

"It's fine with me as long as it's all right with your parents."

Once they had their parents' permission, the kids raced upstairs to grab their gear. It took two trips to move everything from the house to the barn—sleeping bags, pillows, flashlights, a camping lantern, Horse-opoly, water bottles, and snacks. Everyone climbed to the top of the newly stacked hay except Jared and Jessie. They stayed below and threw the sleeping bags and pillows up.

Jessie picked up a battery-powered lantern from the barn floor and cocked her arm to throw it up to Rosie.

"No!" Jared grabbed her arm just in time. "Are you crazy? You could kill someone with that thing."

"We can use that lunge line to pull the bigger stuff up." Rosie pointed to an extra-long nylon lead rope hanging from a hook on the barn wall.

"Perfect." Jared picked up the coiled rope, slipped his arm into the loop and pulled it up over his shoulder. He climbed the stack of hay, then leaned out and tied the line to a rafter. "Okay, Jess. When I drop this down, tie your end to the handle of the lantern. As soon as you're ready, tug on the line, and I'll pull it up."

When Jessie had the rope tied, Jared pulled the lantern up. The girls placed it in the center of the assortment of sleeping bags and switched the light on.

"Turn off the barn lights," Rosie yelled down to Jessie.

The lantern gave off plenty of light in a circle around them, and Rosie could make out the shadowy figures of the horses in their stalls below. She had worried that it might be too hot on top of the hay, but it had cooled down that evening and was quite comfortable in the barn.

"I hope the batteries don't run out," Rosie said. "I should have brought an extra set."

Jared sent the rope back down. "Jess, tie a bucket to that, and put the rest of our stuff in it, then I'll pull it up."

After a couple of bucket loads, they had pulled up the Horse-opoly game, flashlights, snacks, and bottles of water.

Jessie scrambled up the bales to join the others. "I wanted to sleep in the hayloft."

"It's packed full of hay right now," Rosie said. "Maybe this fall we can have a campout up there. After we feed some of the hay, there will be room for us."

As Jared untied the bucket, he looked at the rope attached to the rafters and then down to the ground.

"Oh no." Rosie rolled her eyes. "What are you thinking?"

Jared grinned. "I bet I could swing down on this."

"Yeah, and slam right into Scamper's stall and break every bone in your—" Rosie stopped. That sounded exactly like something her grandmother would say. She wasn't sure whether that was a good or a bad thing.

"I just need to aim down the aisle instead of straight across. Jessie, would you go turn the lights back on for me?"

Jessie scrambled down the stack of hay again and flicked the lights on. The others watched as Jared tied a knot in the line near his hands and another larger one near the bottom for his feet. He moved to the front of the stack of hay and jumped out. After an initial drop of a few feet, he swung back and forth down the aisle.

"Oh wow! That was fun!" Jared slid hand over hand down the rope and dropped to the ground. "You guys gotta try it!"

Rosie was next. "Stand over there, in case I aim wrong." She pointed across the aisle to Scamper's stall.

"Yeah, right," Jared said. "So you can crash into me?" But he went ahead and stationed himself in front of the stall door.

Rosie looked down, turned to what she thought was the right angle, and then jumped. There was an initial free fall as she dropped from the tall stack of hay. The jolt, after the slack in the rope played out, almost caused her to lose her grip, but she held on. She found the lower knot with her feet, which relieved the pressure on her arms, then she was able to relax and enjoy swinging back and forth.

"That *is* fun!" She let go of the rope, dropped to the floor, and ran immediately to the haystack. "I want to do it again."

When they all had their fill of swinging, Rosie got out the Horse-opoly game. "Make sure you keep all the pieces on the sleeping bags. If we drop these little playing pieces in this hay, we'll never find them again."

"And the horses might eat them," Jessie held up her small horseshoe playing piece. "That would be hard on their teeth!"

Several hours into the game, Carrie had purchased most of the horses and owned many barns and stables.

"You've been practicing this, haven't you?" Jared accused her.

"No." Carrie shook her head. "I've never played it before. Oh, by the way, you just landed on my stable." She held out her hand. "You owe me two hundred dollars."

Jared groaned and tossed his last hundred-dollar bills at her.

Jessie rubbed her eyes. "This game is boring."

Jamie elbowed her sister. "You only think it's boring because you're losing."

"No one can beat Carrie now," Lauren said. "Why don't we quit and get some sleep? I'm sure Grandma has a lot planned for us to do tomorrow."

They packed up the game, and everyone stretched out on top of their sleeping bags.

Rosie wiggled around until she found a position where she wasn't being poked by a stalk of hay or someone's elbow. This was only the first day of Cousins Camp, but she didn't see how it could get much better. Rosie switched the lantern off. She could hear the twins breathing heavily already. A horse moved around in the stall below, but she could no longer see either of them. A mosquito buzzed around her face, and she swatted it away.

Suddenly she heard a strange hissing sound behind her. Without looking back, she said. "Jared, knock it off. I'm trying to get to sleep."

"What?" Jared asked sleepily.

Her cousin sure didn't give up easily. She turned around to face him. "You can't fool me. I know you're trying to scare me. Stop making that weird noise."

"What noise?"

SSSS!

This time the sound was louder. Rosie gulped.

"It's probably one of Grandma's cats," Jared said.

"Katy and Jemimah would never hiss at us." Rosie grabbed a flashlight and aimed it at the back wall. She tracked the light along the wall where the sloping roof met the top row of hay bales. She'd almost given up when the light suddenly revealed an ugly creature in the corner with glowing eyes and bared teeth. The animal flicked its tail, opened its mouth wide, and hissed again.

"Aagh!" Rosie screamed and dropped the flashlight. Her heart thumped as she climbed over Carrie. She scrambled over the others who were between her and the way down from the hay.

"What? What's going on?" Carrie asked.

"There's a wild animal over there!" Rosie flung her arm in the direction of the wall behind her, but kept moving forward.

If they had been asleep before, the cousins were definitely awake now—and all trying to climb down the stack of hay at once.

Rosie waited for everyone to make it to the bottom, then she ran down the aisle to the front of the barn. The kids sprinted through the darkness to the house, entering through the laundry room door.

The ruckus apparently woke Grandma in the next room. She stumbled into the hallway, rubbing her eyes. "What are you all doing back inside?"

"There's a wild animal in the barn!" Rosie explained breathlessly. "It was hissing at us and looked like it was ready to attack. Should we wake Dad up? It might hurt the horses."

"Where was it?" Grandma blinked sleepily.

"On top of the hay, by the back wall," Rosie explained.

"What color was it?" Grandma asked between yawns.

"Kind of grayish, and it had huge teeth!"

"How big?"

Rosie frowned. "Its teeth?"

Grandma shook her head. "No. The animal. How big was the animal?"

"I don't know." Rosie shrugged. "About Jemimah's size, I guess."

Grandma laughed.

"What's so funny?" Rosie was surprised that her grandmother wasn't concerned for the horses' safety.

"Sounds like a possum. That's about the only thing that would be up there, other than a raccoon. There's not much danger of a possum attacking the horses,"[1] Grandma said. "I don't suppose you brought your pillows over with you?"

The kids looked at each other and shook their heads.

---

1   Possums may transmit the disease EPM (Equine Protozoal Myeloencephalitis) to horses if the horse's feed is contaminated by possum waste products.

"Go on upstairs and get some sleep. Quietly. No need to wake the whole family." Grandma turned to go back to bed.

Rosie allowed the others to go ahead of her. She watched as they tiptoed up the stairs.

"Haven't you ever seen a possum before?" Jared hissed.

"What? You were scared too," Rosie said in a loud whisper. "If you're so smart, why didn't you tell me it was a possum?"

"I barely saw it. You're the one who screamed like a girl and scared everyone half to death."

"I am a girl!" Rosie glared at her cousin.

At the top of the stairs, the girls turned left, and Jared went right.

Boys. Rosie sighed. *They think they know everything.*

15

Barrels and Barn Painting

W hen the kids tromped down the stairs to breakfast the next morning, Eric greeted them with a big smile. "Come on and have a seat! Grandma's prepared a special dish. I think you'll like it."

"Mmm!" Everything smelled delicious. Rosie's mouth began to water. She could use a good breakfast after last night. Jared had made fun of her again that morning before they came downstairs. He blamed her for ruining their campout.

Grandma carried a large, covered pot to the table and set it on a hot pad.

Eric removed the lid and looked inside. "It's possum stew!" He slapped his knee and laughed so hard Rosie thought he might fall off his chair. Soon all the adults were laughing with him.

"D-a-a-d! It's not funny. That animal was creepy!" Rosie frowned and plunked herself down at the end of the table as far away from her father as she could get. She had never seen him laugh like that.

Grandma placed a large serving spoon in the pot. "No possum stew, but how about some oatmeal?"

Kristy and Lisa added plates of pancakes, eggs, and bacon to the table.

"We'll have Jonathan ask the blessing this morning," Grandma said. "Eric doesn't seem to be capable of praying right now."

Eric did his best to stop laughing. Rosie peeked at him during the prayer and saw him wiping tears from his eyes. She didn't understand what was so funny about a possum.

After Jonathan prayed, Grandma said, "Help yourselves, kids. Today's agenda includes barrel racing and barn painting."

"We're going to race barrels?" Carrie whispered to Rosie.

At first Rosie thought her friend was joking. "Yes, haven't you ever done that before? Someone rolls the barrel, then you run and try to beat it."

Carrie shook her head. "No. Is it hard?"

Rosie smiled. "I'm just kidding. You'll see. You run around the barrels on horseback."

"Oh! That makes more sense."

Although Rosie knew what it was, she had never tried it. Jared and the twins barrel raced, so everyone must be using their three horses today.

After breakfast, Julie led the way to the barn. "This morning we'll use Patches, Pearl, and Scamper to teach you how to barrel race."

What? Did her aunt mean to say Scout instead of Scamper? "My horse doesn't know how to barrel race!" Rosie protested. This day was not getting off to a good start. *What was Aunt Julie thinking, using Scamper for barrel racing?*

Julie was unfazed. "You're right. Scamper doesn't know how to barrel race—and neither do you. I'll use him to show you how we start training barrel horses by first walking and then trotting the pattern."

Jared made a face at Rosie and ran to set up three large barrels. The girls helped Julie saddle the horses and lead them to the arena. Since Julie's kids already knew how to barrel race, they acted as her assistants.

Rosie was selected to go first. She mounted Scamper and guided him toward the starting line at the entrance of the arena. She stopped and looked at the barrel on her left, then shifted in her saddle, and glanced at the other one on the right. "Which way do I go, Aunt Julie?"

"You're allowed to start in either direction. Most people do the right barrel first. Ride to the left of that barrel and circle to the right. Then stay to the right of the next barrel, and circle it to the left. After that go all the way down and circle the farthest barrel. Turn left on that one, also. To finish, come straight down the middle back to where you started from. The pattern looks kind of like a cloverleaf."

Rosie walked Scamper through the pattern the first time, then repeated it at a trot. The pony made large, wide circles around the barrels, especially at the trot. In order to have a fast time, it was important for the horse to circle tightly around each barrel. It was okay for now though. Scamper was still learning. Maybe someday he would become an expert barrel racer.

After each of the kids had taken a few turns practicing the pattern at a walk and trot, Julie asked, "Does anyone want to try Pearl at a canter? She knows how to barrel race already, but she won't go too fast unless you really push her."

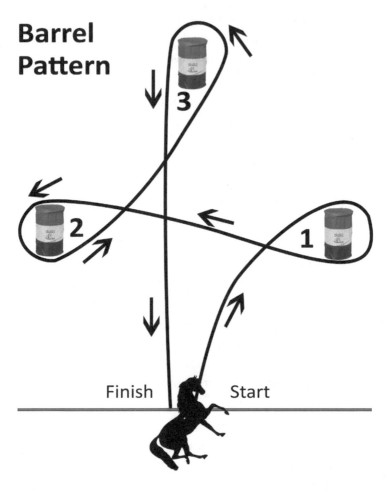

Barrel Pattern

3

2

1

Finish   Start

Carrie and Lauren looked at each other. Rosie could tell they were both afraid to try, so she volunteered. "I'll do it."

"Hold her back a little," Julie instructed as Rosie mounted Jamie's horse. "And—hold on to the horn."

Was Jared watching her? Rosie hadn't held on to the horn since she first started riding, and she didn't want her cousin to think she was a beginner. He wasn't looking her way, so Rosie grabbed the horn with her left hand and steered Pearl with her right.

Pearl cantered toward the first barrel. It was a smooth, comfortable canter, which made Rosie wonder why Julie had told her to hold on. When they came closer to the barrel, Rosie wasn't sure what to do, but it didn't matter—Pearl knew. The horse dug her hooves into the sandy arena and made a sudden, sharp turn to the right, so close that Rosie felt her knee graze the barrel.

Pearl could sure turn fast! Now Rosie understood why Julie had told her to hold on. She gripped the horn more tightly, and a huge smile spread across her face. *This was fun!* She was little more than a passenger as Pearl continued the pattern to the second barrel, then the third, and turned for home. Rosie encouraged the mare to go faster and was thrilled by the horse's burst of speed.

"Well, what do you think?" Julie asked as Rosie stopped back at the starting line. "Ready to start barrel racing Scamper?"

Rosie nodded enthusiastically and hopped off Jamie's horse. The excitement of barrel racing erased the bad mood that had been growing since the possum incident the night before.

"Oh no you don't," Grandma objected. "You're not turning Scamper into a barrel racer—at least not for a few more years. I've seen too many horses ruined by contesting them too early."

"I agree," Julie said. "He's not ready yet, but give him a few more years, and he could be good at it." She nodded to Jessie. "The twins are going to demonstrate how fast these old Paints can go."

Grandma looked around. "Who has the stopwatch?"

Jared pulled it from his pocket and handed it to her. Grandma positioned herself at the starting line, and the kids lined up outside the fence to watch Jessie warm up on Patches.

When Jessie was ready, Julie yelled, "Go!"

Grandma immediately clicked a button on the stopwatch. Patches kicked up sand in the arena as she sped toward the first barrel. She whipped around it with Jessie yelling crazily, urging her to go faster.

"Wow!" That was much faster than she and Pearl had gone. Jessie stuck to her horse like a burr. Rosie had a new respect for her cousin. She would have to stop bringing up how much younger Jessie was. With the head start she had on barrel racing, it would be hard for Rosie to catch up.

Grandma clicked the stopwatch at the precise moment Jessie crossed the finish line. "Twenty point seven seconds!"

Jamie was up next on Pearl. Patches and Pearl were equally fast. This time, though, Jamie finished two tenths of a second faster than Jessie.

"Good job," Jessie congratulated her sister.

Rosie blinked. She had expected Jessie to be angry that Jamie had beaten her, but she was being a good sport about it.

Grandma waved them all toward the barn. "You can ride again tonight, but right now my old barn is long overdue for a fresh coat of paint. After you put the horses up, run to the house and change into your work clothes."

The weathered, white barn was not very big, as far as barns go, but it served Grandma's purposes well. She had enough room for her own horses and had occasionally boarded horses for friends over the years. The two stalls opposite Scamper and Kezzie were now used as hay storage. That way she no longer had to climb the ladder to the hayloft. Rosie and Carrie enjoyed pushing bales down from the loft for Grandma when her supply below ran out. Rosie hadn't noticed it before, but now that she looked more closely, the barn could definitely use a fresh coat of paint.

Everyone split into groups to work on different sides of the barn. Rosie and Carrie grabbed a paint bucket and brushes and walked to the front where they found Jessie squatting down, pulling tall grass and weeds away from the lower boards of the wall.

Rosie set the bucket down and dipped her brush carefully into it.

Carrie stood watching the other two as if she was unsure what to do. "You're good at barrel racing."

Rosie didn't think Carrie knew which twin she was talking to, but it didn't matter. They were both good.

"Thanks." Jessie looked up. "It's fun."

"Too bad Jamie beat you." Rosie couldn't resist teasing her cousin, and she wanted to let Carrie know which twin they were working with.

Jessie threw the weeds in her hand at Rosie.

Carrie splashed white paint on the wall, slapping the brush from side to side. "I like Cousins Camp. It's even fun working, because we're doing it together."

Rosie nodded. "I know. The work is more fun than I thought it would be when Grandma first told us about it."

Carrie dipped her brush deeply into the bucket, and globs of paint dripped from it. When Jessie stood up, Carrie took a quick step toward her and brushed paint down one of the girl's arms.

Jessie squealed and leaped back. "Hey, why did you do that? You're supposed to paint the wall—not me!"

"Oh?" Carrie laughed. "Sorry, but it's not nearly as bad as raw egg in your hair."

Jessie stared at her arm and sputtered.

Rosie and Carrie laughed and ran to the other side of the barn before Jessie had time to avenge herself. Water fights were fun, but a paint fight was not anything Rosie wanted to be part of.

When the painting project was finished that afternoon, Grandma stood back and marveled at the gleaming, white barn. "You've all done a great job! I don't remember it looking this good when it was brand-new."

On Wednesday, Jared helped the men repair the pasture fences while the girls saddled up and rode around the back of the property, through the woods and along the creek.

That afternoon they packed the trucks and trailers with the camping equipment, tack, and supplies they would need for their trail ride the following day. The girls gathered things from their room to carry to the truck.

Rosie couldn't believe that Carrie had never been camping or on a trail ride before. "Here. Take your sleeping bag."

"Who will be in our tent?" Carrie asked.

"All of us girls. You, me, Lauren, Jessie, and Jamie."

Carrie frowned. "I hope Jessie doesn't bring any paint."

"Or eggs!"Rosie started out the bedroom door. "Maybe you two are even now."

117

Carrie followed her down the stairs. "And what do we do with the horses? Is Scamper staying in the tent with us?"

Rosie rolled her eyes. "The horses will be tied to picket lines. You'll see when we get there."

They ran to catch up with Grandma, who was on her way to the barn. Rosie counted in her head. "Grandma, we have thirteen people but only six horses."

"They have horses to rent at the camp," Grandma explained. "You kids will each ride your own, except Carrie will take Scout so Lauren can ride Kezzie, and Jared will use a rental."

"Your mom and dad are riding with us?" Carrie said. "I've never seen them on horses before."

"Rosie's mom is an excellent rider," Grandma said.

"My dad's a beginner, though," Rosie added. "He could be really good, but he doesn't have time to ride much."

Carrie looked nervous. "You'll stay close to me. Won't you?"

Rosie nodded. "Scamper likes to be with Scout." She was so excited; if her arms weren't full, she would have done a cartwheel. "I can't wait till tomorrow! This will be the biggest trail ride I've ever been on."

16
Trail Ride

Rosie's eyes popped open. She looked at the clock on the dresser across the room. Six o'clock. Today was the trail ride! She jumped off her cot and fired her pillow at Carrie's head.

Carrie jumped.

"Come on! Wake up!" Rosie shouted, bouncing around the room. "Wake up all you poofy-heads! Do you want to sleep right through the trail ride?"

Carrie grabbed Rosie's pillow and hurled it back at her. The other girls joined in, bombarding Rosie with pillows. Laughing, she dodged them all and ran out the door and down the stairs.

"Have a seat." Grandma motioned toward the table. She bustled about, cleaning the kitchen. "Did anyone get the ice chests? We won't eat for the next two days if we forget those."

"Eric's putting them in the camper right now," Kristy assured her.

Soon the rest of the kids made it into the kitchen. They gulped down their breakfast and cleared the dishes from the table.

"All that's left is to get the horses in the trailers." Grandma led the way to the barn and supervised while the kids loaded the six horses into two trailers.

They divided up passengers between two trucks and Lisa's car. Rosie, Carrie, and Lauren piled into Grandma's truck, and the caravan pulled out of the drive.

Two minutes down the road Rosie piped up, "Are we there yet?"

The girls burst into laughter.

"I don't know where you got that sense of humor," Grandma remarked wryly.

"From you!" Rosie laughed.

"We have about an hour and a half left of our hour-and-a-half trip. Why don't you girls play a game, and we'll be there before you know it."

"We should have brought Horse-opoly," Carrie said.

"Why, so you could beat us again?" Rosie groaned. "Let's play I Spy."

When the girls tired of that, they invented a new game. They were having so much fun that the time passed quickly.

Carrie was the first to spot the sign for the Diamond C Ranch. "There it is!"

Grandma turned in to the camp entrance and maneuvered the truck and trailer up the steep gravel drive. She pulled alongside Julie's rig in a grove of tall oaks. Soon everyone was busy unloading horses and pitching tents.

The campground was on the edge of a state forest. The large trees provided shade for their campsite. The horses, tied to the trailers, munched hay from their hay bags and watched curiously as the colorful tents were erected.

"You won't catch me in one of those. Sleeping on the ground doesn't agree with my old bones," Grandma announced. "I'll spend the night in my comfortable camper. Anyone who wants to join me is welcome."

Rosie wasn't interested in taking Grandma up on her offer. Her bones weren't old, and she was excited about tent camping. After the campground was set up, they began saddling the horses for their first ride. Jared went with the adults to the camp stable to pick out their rental horses. It was quite a group when everyone was saddled and ready to go.

Carrie looked around at the horses and riders and leaned toward Rosie. "This must be what it felt like to go on a cattle drive in the Old West."

"We have everything but the cows." Rosie grinned. "I know what you mean. I've never ridden with this many people either."

"Since Julie knows these trails," Grandma said, "she'll be our leader. Jonathan will be next, then you kids. The rest of us will fall in behind you."

The trail meandered through hundreds of acres of forest. Going away from camp it was marked by splashes of white paint on trees to the right of the trail. The group was so long from beginning to end that it was impossible to hear anyone more than a few horses away. Messages had to be passed up and down the line.

Carrie and Rosie found themselves in the middle of the pack. Carrie's mount, Scout, and Scamper had become buddies during Cousins Camp and were happy to be together on the trail.

"Deer!" Rosie heard someone ahead of her say. She turned and yelled, "Deer!" to the riders behind her. "Over there, Carrie." She pointed to a doe with twin fawns off to her right.

"Where?"

"On the ridge up there. Don't you see them?" Rosie pointed again.

"Oh, I see them now. They're so cute!"

The deer stood motionless at a safe distance, their big eyes following the long procession. The horses paid no attention to their audience; each was focused on the horse immediately in front of him. As the heat of the day increased, so did the pesky flies, tormenting the horses despite all the fly spray that had been applied to their coats before leaving camp.

The sound of swishing tails, jangly reins, squeaky leather saddles, and buzzing flies merged with hoof beats and the riders' voices to form a sort of trail song in Rosie's ears. She loved horses so much; she sometimes wished she lived before cars were invented, so she could ride Scamper everywhere.

After climbing a steep hill, Rosie glanced to her right and realized she was looking out over the edge of a cliff. Not far from the trail was a rocky outcropping, and beyond that, a drop of about thirty feet into the gorge below. She instinctively steered to the left, as far from the edge as possible.

Carrie followed her. "Scout won't fall over the cliff, will he?"

"No," Rosie spoke loudly so Carrie could hear. "Horses are careful. They won't get too close to the edge, but—I still like to stay as far away as I can."

They started down a steep slope. The horses angled themselves into the hill, bouncing the riders with their short, choppy steps.

Rosie turned to look at Carrie and thought she seemed worried. "Let Scout pick his own way. Lean back a little when you go downhill and forward when you go up."

Carrie loosened her reins and leaned back as Scout continued down the hill.

"Creek crossing!" The message reached the girls from the riders ahead of them. Before she could see it, Rosie heard the gurgling creek.

Everyone along the line stopped and watched Julie urge Elektra toward the clear, sparkling water. The tall Thoroughbred pranced to the left and then to the right to see whether there was any way around; then she stopped and appeared to be trying to decide whether she could jump over to the bank on the other side. Running out of options, she pawed at the water a few times and gingerly placed one leg into the creek. Apparently convinced that it wasn't deep enough to drown in, Elektra stepped into the water and walked calmly across.

By the time the girls reached the creek, the water was so muddy Rosie couldn't see the bottom. Scout and Scamper plunged in and splashed water everywhere. Rosie wiped her face with her sleeve. "Thanks for the shower, Scamp."

About a mile further on, the trail opened up into a grassy clearing with a picnic table. They stopped to eat and give the horses a chance to rest. After lunch, they mounted, and the group started again. Everyone rode in clusters of two or three, talking and laughing together, as they followed the trail that looped back to the campground. When they arrived, Carrie started toward the trailer with Scout.

123

"No, Carrie, we'll put them on the picket line overnight," Rosie said.

"Oh. I thought we'd tie them to the trailer like we did before." Carrie followed Rosie to a line that stretched above the horses' heads, between two wood posts.

While Rosie cared for Scamper, Julie showed Carrie how to tie Scout to the overhead line. "This gives them more freedom to move," she explained. "They can lie down if they want when they're on a picket line, and there's no chance of them getting a leg stuck under the trailer."

After the horses were settled in for the night, the family gathered around a campfire, and Grandma served up her special camp stew.

Eric held out his bowl. "Any possum in this stew?"

"Oh no," Kristy moaned. "Don't start that again."

Rosie grinned at her dad's joke. It was kind of funny that she had been afraid of a possum.

As Eric finished his first bowl of stew and stood up to get a second helping, he flattened one hand against his back and seemed to have trouble moving his legs.

Carrie leaned toward Rosie. "What's wrong with your dad?"

"I'd say four-hour trail rides aren't part of his normal daily routine," Grandma laughed.

They weren't part of Rosie's routine either, but she wished they were. "This stew is great. I'm stuffed!" She swallowed her last bite and patted her stomach. "You know what, Grandma? You haven't told us any stories this week."

"You're right. We've been so busy I haven't had time."

Jamie walked over and sat next to her grandmother. "Can you tell us one now?"

Rosie threw her paper bowl into the fire and pulled Carrie along with her to sit beside her mom and dad. She loved her grandmother's stories, even though she'd heard many of them over and over again.

17

Family Stories

Grandma made herself comfortable in a lawn chair. "Let me see. Have I ever told you about the time I met an angel on the trail?"

The kids looked at each other wide-eyed and shook their heads.

Carrie loved hearing Grandma's stories. She stared at the campfire and listened.

"Kristy and I were on a trail ride with a horse club I belonged to. Kristy was about nine, and riding Ebony—Scamper's grandmother. I was on Ginger, a Missouri Fox Trotter mare I had at the time. Everything was fine at first. Ebony was a scrappy little pony who didn't just keep up with the bigger horses, she usually tried to get ahead of them."

Carrie smiled. She hadn't known Ebony, but she'd been around Scamper enough to know that he had inherited some of his grandmother's personality.

"The trails turned out to be very rocky," Grandma continued. "Ebony and Ginger didn't have shoes on. After several miles, their feet began to get a little sore, and they had a hard time keeping up with the other horses. I felt bad for Ginger and Ebony—and for the rest of the group. We had to go so slow that we were holding everyone back. I told them to go on without us. That way we could take our time getting back to camp. There was one problem with my plan though—I had never ridden those trails before, and they were poorly marked.

"We continued in the direction the group had gone, but they were soon out of sight, and we were on our own. As we rode on and on, I began to worry. It was getting late, and I didn't know how much farther it was to camp—or even if we were headed in the right direction."

Carrie glanced at Rosie's mother. It was hard to imagine her as a kid and Grandma as her mom. Cousins Camp was fun, but at the same time, being around Rosie's family caused a strange pain deep inside her. It made her wonder what *her* mom and grandmother were like. Would she ever know?

"We came to a fork in the trail and stopped. We'd been riding for so long; I thought we had to be getting close to camp. I pulled out my map but couldn't tell where we were. No matter which way I turned, it looked the same. All I saw were trees, trees, and more trees. I was tired and trying hard not to let Kristy see the panic I was beginning to feel."

"You did a good job, because I never noticed anything was wrong," Kristy said. "It just seemed like any other trail ride we'd been on."

"I'm glad. I didn't want to frighten you," Grandma said, then continued with her story. "We sat there for quite some time while I tried to figure out which way to turn. I had just decided to take the right fork of the trail when I heard a rider coming up behind us.

"It was a man on a large sandy-colored mule. He must have noticed that I had my map out. 'Need any help?' he asked kindly. I explained that we were trying to get back to the campground. 'That's where I'm heading. Follow me.' He rode past, and we started after him. When I saw him turn to the *left*, my heart gave a thud, and I whispered a prayer of thanks." Grandma grew quiet and stared at the fire.

Carrie wondered what Grandma's story meant. Was she saying the man on the mule was an angel? Didn't angels glow and have large wings? It seemed that you'd know right away if you had seen an angel.

"Aw, Grandma. That's it? That's the end of the story? You think that guy was an angel?" Jessie poked at the fire with a long stick, sending sparks flying up into the dark sky.

"Jessie, put the stick down," Eric said.

Jessie reluctantly tossed the stick into the fire. "An angel wouldn't ride a mule. They'd ride a dazzling white stallion!"

"Maybe he was—maybe he wasn't," Grandma said. "All I know is that he came along at exactly the moment we needed him. The Bible says we can 'entertain angels unawares,'[1] meaning that sometimes angels are around us, and we don't even know it. If we had turned to the right as I had decided, who knows where Kristy and I would have ended up? With darkness approaching and two footsore horses, we probably would have had to spend the night alone in the forest."

Eric threw another log on the fire. "That reminds me of the verse that says, 'There is a way that seems right to a man, but its end is the way of death.'"[2]

---

1   Hebrews 13:2
2   Proverbs 14:12 NKJV

Rosie jerked her head toward her father. "Are you saying Mom and Grandma might have died out there?"

"No." Eric shook his head. "Just that when we follow our own way, it doesn't turn out well. It's much better to follow God's way."

Grandma nodded in agreement. "Does anyone else have a story?"

Rosie walked over and whispered something to her Uncle Robert.

He looked puzzled. "Lisa, I don't have any idea what she's talking about, but Rosie wants me to ask you whether you ever found your swimming suit."

Rosie grinned and ran back to sit beside her mother.

"Oh, not that story again," Lisa groaned. "Yes, I did find my swimming suit, Rosie. But I have to confess I never learned to dive into the pool."

Robert seemed more confused. "Pool? What are you talking about?"

Lisa waved away his question. "I'll explain it some other time. I have a better story. This was on our first ride at Alum Creek State Park. Julie was five, and she was riding with Mom on Ginger. Kristy and I were behind them on my horse, Maggie. We were surprised by how steep some of the ravines were on the trail. Mom and Julie made it down the first hill, but when Maggie started down, her saddle slid way forward, and I ended up on her neck. Kristy and I yelled, but Mom didn't stop."

"It sounded like you two were laughing," Grandma replied. "I thought you were just having fun."

"When Mom noticed we weren't following her any more, she turned around. She and Julie both laughed at the sight of me perched on Maggie's neck with Kristy hanging on for dear life to my waist."

Carrie watched Rosie laugh at her aunt's story. She was happy for her but envious at the same time. Normally she didn't allow herself to think about her parents, but now she couldn't push back the painful feelings. It made her feel sad even though everyone surrounding her was happy. How was it possible to miss someone so much, that she had never really known?

"Mom thought the saddle was loose," Kristy went on, "so we got off while she tightened it. Then we all got back on."

"The next time we went down a hill, the same thing happened," Lisa said, "but this time Mom was watching."

"What did you do, Aunt Lisa?" Jamie asked.

"For the rest of that trail ride, we stopped when we reached the top of each hill. Kristy and I would jump off and lead Maggie down, then we'd stop at the bottom to get back on. Mom's horse, Ginger, learned to stop when she reached the bottom of a hill. She would look back toward us to see whether we were on Maggie before she started walking again."

"We got nearly as much exercise as Maggie did that day," Kristy added. "After that trip, Mom bought a breeching to keep the saddle from sliding forward on hilly rides. Maggie hated that thing. I think she was embarrassed to wear it. Someone must have told her that breechings are usually used on mules."

Carrie leaned toward Rosie and whispered, "What's a breeching?"

Rosie whispered back, "A leather strap that goes around their hindquarters and attaches to the saddle."

They all sat quietly for a few minutes, then Grandma thought of another story. "Lisa, remember when you and I were riding the Maple Glen trail? It was an out-and-back trail, and we'd never ridden all the way to the end before. We were within a half-mile of our goal one day when Maggie began to limp."

"Yeah," Lisa said. "We both got off, and you checked her hoof. There didn't seem to be anything wrong, but Maggie refused to put any weight on that leg."

"I was disappointed that, once again, we weren't going to reach the end of the trail," Grandma said, "but even worse, I had no idea how to get a lame horse five miles back to the trailer."

"We turned around, and Maggie almost immediately began to perk up," Lisa said. "Five minutes later, I had a hard time keeping her from trotting. She showed no signs of being lame at all."

Grandma nodded. "I'm still convinced that sneaky horse faked the whole thing, so we would go back to the trailer."

Lisa laughed. "Since it got her out of work that time, Maggie tried the limping routine again on the next ride, but we were onto her trick after that."

Rosie looked around. "What about you, Aunt Julie? Do you have a horse story?"

"All I know is that I was the only one to fall off any of our horses. I must have fallen off Ebony a dozen times, but fortunately, it wasn't far to the ground. I guess I shouldn't have tried riding her bareback—with no bridle or halter."

As they all laughed, Kristy leaned back in her chair. "Carrie?"

Carrie sat staring at the fire and didn't respond.

Rosie waved her hand in front of Carrie's face. "Anybody in there?"

"What?" Carrie turned suddenly toward Rosie as if coming out of a trance.

"You've been awfully quiet," Kristy said. "Of course, with this noisy bunch, it's hard to get a word in edgewise. Would you like to share those deep thoughts with us?"

"Umm," Carrie hesitated. *Rosie is so lucky to have a family like this. I don't even know who my parents are. Why does Grandma have angels helping her and I don't? And why can't I ever seem to say what it is I'm feeling?*

Carrie could sense everyone staring at her. All she could think of to say was, "You have a nice family."

Kristy put her arm around Carrie. "Since you're an honorary cousin now, I guess that makes you an official member of this big, crazy family."

18

Draw Me Close To You

Carrie leaned against Kristy's side. The Jacksons weren't her *real* family, but it was fun to pretend that they were.

Lisa stood and pulled out a large, black case from behind her chair. She took out her guitar and strummed a praise song. Everyone sang along. When that one ended, someone called out another title.

Carrie loved to sing. She wasn't familiar with all the songs, but she joined in on the ones she knew.

"One last song," Lisa announced. "Draw me close to You," she began, and everyone joined in.

"Never let me go."

Carrie knew this song, but for the first time she began to think about the meaning of the words. Grandma's story about Satin rejecting Kezzie popped into her mind. She remembered Grandma saying that God was the Father who would never abandon her.

"You're all I want," the song continued. "You're all I've ever needed. Help me know You are near."

Carrie was surprised to feel tears forming in her eyes. She quickly brushed them away and looked around to see whether anyone was watching. Her heart was beating so rapidly it frightened her. *Is that You, God? Are You really here?*

She didn't hear a voice, but something stirred in her heart. Places inside that she had kept tightly closed for years, began to unfold like a flower's petals in the warm morning sun. She stared at the fire. *What was happening to her?*

"Come on, Carrie." Rosie tapped her on the shoulder. "Everyone's going to bed."

Carrie jumped. The others were leaving the campfire.

"Are you all right?" Rosie shined her flashlight toward Carrie's face. "You're sure acting strange tonight."

Carrie blinked, throwing her hands up in front of her face to block the glaring light. "I'm okay." She silently followed the rest of the girls to the tent.

"I'll be right next door if you need anything." Kristy zipped the tent shut when the girls were all inside. "Don't stay up too long."

"Don't worry, Mom. I'm beat." Rosie yawned, unrolled her sleeping bag, and stretched out on top of it. Lauren, the twins, and Carrie arranged themselves around Rosie in the small three-person tent. It was a tight fit, but none of the girls were very big. Soon after they prayed together, it grew quiet.

Carrie raised her head and looked around. It seemed everyone was asleep but her. She lay back again, eyes wide open, staring at the stars through the small mesh window in the top of the tent. *God, are You out there? Do You really care about me?*

136

She loved her foster parents, Judy and Ross, but it wasn't the same. Why couldn't she have a father like Rosie did, without the 'foster' part in front of it? Was God really the Father she had always wanted?

She heard Rosie breathing deeply beside her. "Rosie," she whispered.

More deep breathing.

She tried again, poking at her friend's shoulder. "Rosie."

"What?" Rosie answered groggily.

"Are you asleep?"

"Could I answer you if I was asleep?" Rosie rolled over toward Carrie and propped her head up on her elbow. "What's wrong? Do you have to go to the bathroom?"

"No, it's not that. Remember when you told me about your pony, Jet? How she died saving Scamper's life. You said it was like Jesus dying for us."

Rosie nodded.

"I understand it now. I felt God close to me tonight, like the song says." Carrie scooted over beside Rosie and leaned forward so their heads were almost touching. She quietly explained the way she had felt when sitting by the campfire.

"Did you pray?"

"No." Carrie shook her head. "Pray about what?"

"When you decide to follow Jesus, you're supposed to say a prayer."

"What do I say?"

"Tell God you're sorry for your sins and that you accept Jesus as your Lord and Savior."

Carrie wanted to do everything properly, so she bowed her head, and Rosie did the same.

"Dear God, I'm sorry for all the bad things I've done. Thank you, Jesus, for dying on the cross for my sins. I want to follow You now. Thank you, God, for being my real Father." Carrie sniffed and wiped away the tears that came to her eyes. She waited for a moment until she could speak again, then added, "Amen."

Rosie looked up.

"Was that okay?" Carrie asked.

"Perfect." Rosie hugged Carrie and lay back down. "Mom and Dad and Grandma and I have been praying for you for a long time. I'm so glad you're a Christian now."

"I feel kind of the same, but different too. It feels like Christmas Eve—you know, when you're so excited right before something fun happens."

Rosie yawned and nodded.

Carrie stared out the tent window at a star that was shining brightly against the dark sky. She smiled. It felt good to have her very own Father now.

"Goodnight, Rosie."

There was no answer.

The aroma of freshly-brewed coffee, eggs, and bacon drifted through the air as Rosie and Carrie marched arm-in-arm to the breakfast table the next morning. Grandma glanced up from a pan of scrambled eggs she was stirring. The girls stopped in front of her and stood silently.

Grandma paused and looked at them more closely. "What have you two been up to? You don't usually have such big grins this early in the morning."

Carrie beamed, but didn't say a word.

"Don't you notice anything different?" Rosie asked.

Eric and Kristy walked over and stood on either side of Grandma.

"Let's see. You haven't dyed your hair, and you're too old to lose a tooth," Grandma said.

"You swapped clothes?" Kristy guessed.

The girls shook their heads.

Eric shrugged. "We give. What's the big secret?"

"Carrie became a Christian last night!" Rosie blurted out the news before Carrie had a chance to speak. "I thought you'd be able to tell just by looking at her."

"Oh, Carrie, that's wonderful!" Grandma dropped her spatula and hurried around the table to give her a hug. "I'm so happy for you!"

"You should have woken us up last night to tell us," Kristy said.

The rest of the family gathered around to congratulate Carrie. She was embarrassed by all the attention. The warmth she felt spreading over her face matched the warm feeling in her heart.

They sat down to breakfast, and Eric prayed. He thanked God for the food, their family, and the horses, but most of all for the miracle of Carrie's salvation.

Carrie didn't know how it could get much better than this—with Rosie as her best friend, being able to spend time with Rosie's family, and now becoming a Christian. She was smiling so broadly that it was hard to eat her breakfast.

After another day of riding and hiking the trails around the campground, they packed everything up and returned to Sonrise Stable. Carrie was sad that Cousins Camp had come to an end. Her new friend, Lauren, left that evening with her parents to return to Texas.

Everyone had enjoyed the week so much that they agreed Cousins Camp should become an annual event—and Carrie was invited to join them.

19
County Fair

R osie plunged the sponge into the bucket of sudsy water and sighed. "It sure is hard to keep Scamper clean."

The girls were bathing the horses in preparation for taking them to the county fair.

"You're lucky—Kezzie only has that narrow stripe on her face. Scamper's patches and stockings always look dingy. He seems to like being dirty."

"I'll help you in a minute." Carrie ran a comb through Kezzie's wet mane. "I'm kind of nervous about the show. I've never been in a real horse show before—only the Egg and Spoon race we had a few weeks ago at Cousin's Camp. And I wasn't very good at that."

Rosie paused with her hand on Scamper's neck. Soapy water from the sponge dripped down her arm. "You'll do fine. Kezzie's been shown so many times, she's an old pro at it. This will be my first show with Scamper, so I'm kind of nervous too."

Carrie frowned. "I wish my mom, I mean Mrs. Judy, could come to watch me, but she gets tired so easily, she doesn't think she'll be able to make it, and Mr. Ross has to work."

Rosie felt sad for her friend. She couldn't imagine not having any family there when she showed Scamper. "I'm sorry, Carrie. My dad will record the show. Your parents can watch that. And Mom, Aunt Julie, and her kids will be there to cheer for both of us."

"It's okay." Carrie wiped the wet comb off on her jeans and dropped it into the tack bucket. "Where do you need help with this dirty boy?"

After the two scrubbed Scamper until his white patches sparkled, Grandma inspected their work. "Those are certainly two prize-winning horses!"

"I hope so." Rosie walked around, examining her horse one last time. Scamper had to look his best for the fair. She had already picked out a spot for the trophy she hoped to win—right beside one her mom had won with Ebony.

Grandma waved the girls toward the horse trailer that was parked by the barn. "Let's get them loaded and over to the fairgrounds. They're supposed to be in their stalls before seven tonight."

Rosie looked at the truck and trailer—overflowing with tack boxes, a wheelbarrow, hay bales, buckets, grain, saddle racks, pitchforks, and more—everything she and Carrie needed to ride and care for the horses during fair week. She hoped they hadn't forgotten anything.

Scamper hopped into the trailer after Kezzie, then she and Carrie climbed into the back seat of the truck. They were on their way!

Fifteen minutes later, they pulled through the gates at the entrance to the fairgrounds. Butterflies began to flit around in Rosie's stomach. She enjoyed the fair, but she wasn't sure how Scamper would react to all the commotion.

Grandma slowed to a stop, rolled down her window, and handed the horses' health papers to the livestock inspector. He glanced over them, handed them back, and waved them on without saying a word. Grandma drove slowly on the narrow gravel road that wound around the fairgrounds and found a space to park near the horse arena.

When she jumped out of the truck, it seemed that Rosie had entered another world. Everyone on the fairgrounds was busy doing something or rushing somewhere. People continued to pour in, driving all sorts of vehicles—from rattle-trap rusty pickups to gleaming duallies with shiny aluminum trailers—bringing in livestock of every kind: tiny bantam chickens to huge draft horses.

Rosie smiled at the clamor of animal voices—mooing, crowing, gobbling, oinking, and whinnying. It sounded like the animals were as excited about the fair as she was.

Carnival workers were still assembling the Ferris wheel. It looked funny without its top half. The midway rides didn't appeal much to Rosie. Although she didn't like to admit it, many of them scared her, especially the ones that flipped people upside down. And the ones that weren't scary, sometimes upset her stomach. It was more fun to ride Scamper.

One thing did have the power to lure her from the livestock area of the fairgrounds—the food on the midway. She liked it all, but barbecued, shredded-chicken sandwiches were her favorite. She sniffed and smiled. It was starting to smell like dinnertime.

Carrie poked Rosie in the side. "What do we do now?"

Rosie jumped and turned her attention back to their truck and trailer. "Oh, yeah. Let's get the horses into their stalls."

The girls unloaded and led Scamper and Kezzie into adjoining stalls in a big blue-and-white tent similar to the ones used for circuses. There were three horse barns on the grounds, but there were so many entries that the additional horses would be housed in the rented tent. Rosie would have rather been in a barn, but the tent would have to do.

They spread shavings for bedding and gave the horses hay and water. "That stall on the corner is a tack stall." Rosie pointed to her right. "We'll share it with the kids who have horses next to us. Let's get our saddles from the truck and put them in there."

They returned a few minutes later, each carrying a saddle on her hip.

"Outta my way!" A tall, thin teenage boy darted into the tack stall ahead of them and placed his saddle right where Rosie had planned to put hers.

"That's *my* spot," he warned her.

"Um, hi, Billy." Rosie remembered him from the previous year's fair. She motioned to Carrie. "We can put our stuff in the other corner."

Carrie followed Rosie back toward the truck to unload more equipment. "Who was that? He sure was grumpy."

"Billy King." Rosie rolled her eyes. "He's a good rider but not the friendliest person in the world. He won the Pony Pleasure class last year on Bandit. I'll have to beat him if Scamper and I are going to win our trophy."

"At least you and I won't compete against each other, since Kezzie shows in the Easy-Gaited class."

144

"Maybe we'll both take home trophies this year." Rosie handed Carrie a bridle and a pair of boots.

Carrie shrugged. "I just hope I get through the class without messing up. I don't want Grandma to be disappointed after she's spent so much time teaching me."

"Grandma won't be disappointed. She always says it's not about winning. It's about doing your best."

"I'll try to remember that."

Rosie searched through the truck one last time to see whether there was anything else that needed to go into the tack stall.

When they entered the tent, Rosie looked around for Billy, but he was already gone.

Carrie dropped her boots and riding helmet in the tack stall and looped Kezzie's bridle over the saddle horn. "Now what?"

"Let's look around at the animals, then we'll come back and ride." Rosie led Carrie on a tour of the grounds. The fair wasn't officially open yet, so the only people that were there were other exhibitors. The girls avoided the amusement rides and wandered through the sheep and cattle barns on the opposite side of the fairgrounds, stopping to talk to a few friends who had brought animals to the fair. By the time they returned, several riders were already practicing in the arena. The girls saddled up and led their horses out to join them.

"You'll have it easy." Rosie opened the gate, and they entered the arena. "Kezzie's been here before, so she won't even blink at the rides."

Rosie closed the gate behind them and mounted Scamper. "This is all new to him. Most people don't have a Ferris wheel on their farms to practice near—not even Grandma."

"That's an idea." Carrie smiled. "We could put it right beside the barn."

Rosie watched to see how Scamper would react to the other horses in the arena. His head was higher than usual, but he was listening for Rosie's signals. She looked over at Carrie. "What did you say? Put what?"

"The Ferris wheel! We can put it right beside Grandma's barn!"

Rosie shook her head. "You're crazy. Why don't you suggest that to her when we're done? At least the rides don't start running until tomorrow. Scamper doesn't even notice them now, but when they're moving and their lights are flashing, he'll probably think an awful monster is after him."

"We have a whole day before the show," Carrie said. "Maybe if you ride him enough, he'll realize the Ferris wheel monster won't hurt him!"

When Rosie saw her parents walk up to the arena gate, she trotted Scamper over to them. "Hi, Mom. Hi, Dad."

Eric put a foot on the bottom board of the fence and leaned forward placing both arms over the top rail. "How's our boy behaving?"

"Good so far. But I'm kind of worried about the carnival rides starting tomorrow."

Eric rubbed Scamper's forehead between his eyes. "You'll be brave. Won't you, buddy?"

"I could ride him first tomorrow," Kristy offered.

Rosie knew her mom was a better rider, but this was something she wanted to do herself. He was her horse after all. "Thanks, Mom, but I want to try it."

"Okay. Hurry up and finish your ride so we can go home," Kristy said. "We'll have to be back here bright and early tomorrow morning."

Rosie patted her stomach. "What about dinner? I think some of the concession stands are already open. It certainly smells like it."

"We'll grab a quick peanut butter sandwich when we get home."

"Aw, Mom. I was thinking about something more healthy and nourishing."

"Like one of your favorite shredded-chicken sandwiches?"

Rosie grinned and nodded. She could taste the tangy barbecued chicken already.

"Tomorrow," Kristy promised.

20
Billy and Bandit

After they settled the horses in for the night, Carrie went home with Rosie and her family. She was spending the week with them since the girls would be together at the fair most of the time.

Rosie and Carrie were too excited to sleep much that night. When they arrived back at the horse tent early the next morning, Scamper and Kezzie nickered their greetings, happy to see familiar faces, and eager for their breakfast. Rosie patted Scamper as she tossed two flakes of hay into his stall.

"The rides don't open until noon," Kristy said. "Why don't you wait until then to get the horses out?" She put her hand on Rosie's shoulder. "If you change your mind, I can ride him first to see how he reacts. He'll need to get used to the rides before your drill team performs tonight."

Kristy had choreographed a pattern on horseback to music. Rosie, Carrie, and several other members of the 4-H club had practiced it the past few weeks until both they and the horses had all the moves memorized. Rosie looked forward to their performance that evening.

After they finished cleaning the stalls, Rosie and Carrie wandered around the fairgrounds. They spent a lot of time looking at the photography and art exhibits.

Rosie examined several horse sketches in the youth art section. "I have a drawing of Scamper I want to enter next year."

"You're so good at drawing. I'm sure you'll win first place. I can't even draw stick figures." Carrie sighed. "I'm much better at writing."

"I'm awful at writing."

"Anyone can write," Carrie said. "It's like talking, only on paper. I'm better at writing than talking. You and Grandma are easy to talk to, but with most people my mind goes totally blank, and I can't think of anything to say."

Rosie laughed. "I never have that problem, but when I try to write something down, it doesn't sound the same."

Carrie lowered her voice to a whisper. "I write in my diary every night."

Rosie nodded. *Why was Carrie whispering?* She made it sound as if the diary was a deep dark secret.

"I'm working on a story about Kezzie too," Carrie added.

"Oh, wow! That gives me an idea," Rosie said. "You could write a book about horses, and I'll illustrate it."

"That's a great idea! We can use some of the money we make to buy Grandma that indoor riding arena she's always wanted."

Rosie was so excited about the book, she wanted to start on it right away. "What kind of stuff are you writing about Kezzie? I need to know that so I know what pictures to draw."

When they reached the end of the art building, Rosie heard music coming from the carousel. "The carnival rides are starting!"

"Ready to ride Scamper?" Carrie asked.

Rosie gulped. "Uh… I can't find my swimming suit. Um—I mean, I can't find my helmet." She turned to look all around her. "Oh no! I can't find my pony!"

The girls looked at each other and laughed so loudly that people in the building turned to stare at them.

"I can't believe I was such a scaredy-cat about that." Rosie pulled Carrie's arm, and they ran out of the building.

When they reached the horse tent, Rosie patted Bandit as she walked past him to Scamper's stall. She hoped they didn't run into Billy again. She hadn't seen him all morning, but his pony had been fed. Maybe Billy planned to ride later in the day. She and Carrie groomed and saddled Scamper and Kezzie, and led them to the riding arena.

Kristy watched from outside the fence. "Be careful, Rosie. He may be a little skittish."

Rosie nodded and mounted Scamper. He behaved perfectly—until they reached the end of the arena closest to the rides. Just then, one called "The Bullet" turned a group of girls upside down, and they began to scream.

Scamper jerked his head up and leaped sideways. Rosie hung precariously from the side of his neck for a moment. She grabbed the horn and pulled herself back into the saddle. *Whew! That was a close call.* Rosie could feel her heart pounding. She had never fallen off a horse before, and she didn't want to start now. Maybe she should have let her mom ride him first.

151

Scamper snorted and whirled around to face the metal contraption that screamed like a girl. He appeared to be considering whether he should bolt for the other end of the arena, far away from the scary creature.

Rosie saw him look over at Kezzie, who was paying no attention at all to the carnival rides. Scamper snorted loudly, like a wild mustang warning the herd of danger.

Kristy hurried down the outside of the fence toward them. "Are you all right? Are you sure you don't want me to ride him?"

"Yeah. I'm okay, Mom. I think the worst is over. When he realizes Kezzie's not worried, he should settle down."

The chestnut mare resumed plodding calmly around the ring. Scamper pranced behind her, looking back every few steps to see whether the monster was catching up to him.

"Easy, boy. Trust me. It's nothing to be afraid of." Grandma had told her that a horse could sense when his rider was scared. Rosie took a deep breath and tried to relax. She was patient but firm, keeping Scamper moving in as straight a line as possible. After a half dozen laps, he seemed to realize he was not in any danger, and she could feel him calming down.

"Whew! I hope we have that fear conquered." Rosie sighed with relief. "I should teach him that verse Grandma told us—about God not giving us a spirit of fear." She continued working him at a trot and canter to use up the rest of his nervous energy.

Kristy took Scamper's reins when Rosie stopped at the arena gate. "You handled him really well. Do you think he'll be all right tonight?"

Rosie nodded. "He'll be fine. He doesn't seem afraid now."

That evening Rosie and Carrie rode side by side leading the drill team into the arena. Scamper, Kezzie, and the rest of the horses performed flawlessly, weaving and circling in time to the music. The high point of the performance was when they rotated around the center of the arena creating a giant horse pinwheel. The crowd cheered as the team members exited at the end of the routine.

Rosie was surprised to see her aunt Julie making her way through the crowd toward them.

"Great job!" Julie said as Rosie and Carrie rode out of the arena.

"Thanks! I thought you guys weren't coming until tomorrow," Rosie said.

The twins walked up beside their mother. Rosie's mouth watered when Jamie pulled a big wad of pink cotton candy from a plastic bag and stuffed it into her mouth. Rosie wasn't surprised to see that Jessie was empty-handed. The girl had probably eaten all of hers already.

Scamper stretched his neck out and bumped Jamie's shoulder.

"Look out!" Rosie pulled her horse's head back. "Scamper will steal your cotton candy. He might eat the whole thing— plastic bag and all."

Julie unwrapped a mint and fed it to Scamper. "The girls and I are staying to watch the barrel racing. You two want to join us?"

"Sure! We'll have to put these guys in their stalls first." Rosie couldn't wait until she could start training Scamper for barrel racing. She wished Julie's family lived closer. The fair would be even more fun if Jared and the twins were there with Carrie and her.

Julie located another mint and fed it to Kezzie. "Do you need any help, Rosie?"

"No thanks." Rosie jumped down from Scamper. "We'll be back as soon as we take care of them."

The girls led Scamper and Kezzie toward the horse tent, but they ran into a traffic jam of exhibitors and spectators. Rosie turned Scamper around. "Let's go the other way. It'll be faster."

Carrie nodded and followed Rosie.

CRACK!

Scamper jumped sideways as they approached the corner of the horse tent. Rosie jumped also. She turned and looked back at Carrie. "What was that?"

CRACK!

There it was again. Rosie stepped forward and peeked around the corner. She was shocked to see Billy King hitting his pony, Bandit, with a whip. Even though the boy was older and nearly twice her size, Rosie yelled and started to run toward him. "What are you doing?"

Scamper stopped dead in his tracks, refusing to budge. He stared warily at Billy and the whip.

"None of your business, twerp," Billy sneered. "He needed to learn a lesson, that's all."

Rosie was so mad she couldn't think clearly. "I'm telling my grandma how you were treating Bandit!"

"I'm s-o-o scared; I'm shaking in my boots. Oh, no! Granny will get me!" Billy shook his whole body as if he were badly frightened, then laughed and sauntered off, spurs jangling.

When Bandit hesitated, Billy jerked the reins and dragged the trembling pony along behind him.

Rosie's arms shook as she led Scamper into the tent and turned him loose in his stall.

"Poor Bandit," Carrie said. "What a beautiful pony. I can't believe his owner is so mean to him."

"As soon as we're done, let's find Grandma. She'll know what to do about Billy."

Carrie nodded. "I hope so. That guy doesn't deserve a pony like Bandit."

When the girls located Grandma, Rosie's anger returned as a picture of the frightened pony flashed back into her mind. She could hardly speak, so Carrie explained that they had seen Billy whipping his pony.

"That's awful! If he treats Bandit that way here, I can only imagine what he does to him when no one is around." Grandma shook her head. "I'll talk to Billy, but I don't know whether it will make any difference. I could tell his 4-H advisor—or someone on the fair board." Grandma seemed to be thinking out loud. "I'll see what I can do, girls."

Rosie felt better. She was still mad at Billy, but she trusted that her Grandmother would figure out a way to fix everything.

21
Horse Show

A small army assembled early the next morning to help Rosie and Carrie prepare for the show: Kristy and Eric, Julie, Jonathan, their three kids, and of course, Grandma. The morning passed quickly in a flurry of activity as they clipped, bathed, and groomed Kezzie and Scamper.

"I don't think these horses have ever looked this good," Grandma pronounced when they were finished.

"Now it's your turn." Kristy pointed to Rosie and Carrie. "Your show clothes are in the camper. Go wash up and change while we saddle the horses for you. Julie went to sign you up for your classes."

Julie returned to the tent with the exhibitor numbers as Carrie and Rosie arrived in their show outfits.

"Whoo-ee, look at you two!" Julie stepped back and admired the girls. Rosie wore black chaps and a bright purple shirt. Carrie had tan chaps and a green show shirt. "It won't matter how the horses do; you're sure to win first place just for those outfits."

Rosie and Carrie looked at each other and laughed. Kristy pulled out her camera and snapped a few photos of the girls together.

Grandma rolled her eyes. "When I was a kid, everyone showed in blue jeans and white shirts. Horse shows are nothing but fashion contests anymore. It should be about how you ride and how well you've trained and cared for your horse, not how fancy you look."

"They're on class eight now." Kristy examined the show bill. "Carrie, you're in class thirteen, and Rosie is in fifteen. You two better scoot! You need to warm the horses up before your classes.""

The girls turned to leave.

"Hold on!" Julie waved two white paper rectangles with large black numbers printed on one side. "Don't go without these." She pinned Rosie's number on the back of her shirt, while Grandma did the same for Carrie.

"Do your best," Grandma reminded them as she and the rest of the family walked toward the bleachers.

Rosie and Carrie led Scamper and Kezzie to the practice arena not far from the show ring. It was already crowded with contestants warming up for their classes. Once inside the gate, the girls mounted.

"Nervous?" Rosie asked.

Carrie gave a grim smile. "Yeah, what about you?"

"A little." Rosie urged Scamper into a jog, and Carrie followed her.

Soon the announcer called class thirteen, Easy-Gaited Pleasure, to the arena.

"That's you, Carrie."

Carrie stopped Kezzie and stared at Rosie as if unsure what to do.

Rosie gestured toward the show ring. "What are you waiting for? Get in there!"

Carrie rushed toward the gate to enter the class.

Rosie rode to the side of the arena and parked Scamper where she had a good view of the class. She waved to her mom and grandmother in the stands and saw her dad pull out his video camera. She turned back toward the class. *Carrie needs to smile. She looks so nervous.* Rosie tried to catch her attention, but Carrie never looked her way.

Kezzie didn't appear nervous at all. She seemed to love the attention of the crowd.

"Show gait," the announcer called.

Kezzie sped up into a natural, high-stepping running walk. She was so smooth; Carrie barely moved in the saddle.

Rosie leaned forward and patted Scamper's neck. "Your friend looks good, doesn't she, buddy? Grandma always says Kezzie loves an audience. What about you? I hope you'll do that well when it's our turn." Rosie glanced at the horsehair bracelet on her wrist and thought about Jet. "Your mom would be proud of you, Scamper."

The contestants reversed direction and performed the walk and show gait again. At the end of the class, they lined up in the middle of the arena. The judge walked down the line, examining each of the horses, and jotting notes on his clipboard. When he reached the end, he handed the paper he'd been writing on, to the ringmaster who took it to the announcer's booth.

"In sixth place," the announcer began, "number 179, Tim Miller on Smoke 'Em."

Rosie held her breath while they went through the placings: fifth, fourth, third, second …

"And your first-place winner is number 229, Keziah's Jubilee, ridden by Carrie Rogers."

"Yay!" Rosie yelled so loudly that Scamper jumped. "Oops, sorry, boy. I'm just happy because Carrie and Kezzie won!"

Grandma and Kristy rushed to the end of the arena where Carrie, wearing a huge smile, exited with Kezzie.

Carrie stopped beside Scamper and handed Grandma the trophy and large blue ribbon. "I can't believe we won!"

Rosie smiled. "Congratulations, Carrie. You were great!"

"Both of my girls did a great job!" Grandma alternated between patting Carrie's leg and Kezzie's neck. "Let's get Kezzie to her stall so we can watch Rosie's class."

As class fourteen entered the ring, Rosie went back to the makeup arena. Her class was coming up next. She walked Scamper around to keep him loose and relaxed. It wasn't long before the announcer called out, "Class fifteen, Western Pony Pleasure, to the arena."

While she waited at the gate to enter, Rosie saw Carrie and Grandma climb the bleachers to join the rest of the family. She looked over the other contestants. It was hard to tell just by looking at them who might have a chance of beating her. She spotted Billy King a few horses back on Bandit. The palomino gleamed like polished gold. Billy glanced at her, and she made a face at him. She couldn't understand how he could be so mean to Bandit.

When the rider ahead of her started through the gate, Rosie nudged Scamper to follow. Once inside the arena, Rosie turned almost immediately to the left and crossed the arena to get a better position on the rail. Her mom and grandmother had drilled it into her that she needed to stay away from a pack of horses. That way the judge would have a clear view of her and her horse. That worked because she wanted to stay far away from Billy anyway. *Okay,* she told herself. *Forget about Billy for now and concentrate on the class.*

"Jog," The announcer called out a change in gait.

"Jog," Rosie repeated softly to Scamper. She squeezed both legs lightly against his sides. The pony obediently picked up an easy jog. *Stay on the rail,* Rosie reminded herself. She glanced around and didn't see anyone close to her. "Good boy," she whispered to Scamper.

"Lope your ponies."

Rosie applied light rein pressure to tip Scamper's nose inward and pressed with her outside heel. He exploded into a fast canter on the left lead. *Easy, boy. You don't have to get that excited about it.* She pulled back, and Scamper settled into a smooth lope.

After reversing directions, they walked and then jogged to the right. The class was almost over. With her attention focused so intently on Scamper, she wasn't sure how the other riders were doing, but she knew Scamper had performed well enough to win the class. Rosie realized she was holding her breath. She released it and took a deep breath.

The announcer asked for a final lope.

Rosie noticed the judge up ahead. *Don't blow it now, Scamp.*

As she gave the signal for the lope, a blur of horse and rider passed by on her left, then cut directly in front of them. When the other horse's hindquarters brushed against his nose, Scamper tossed his head and swished his tail angrily.

What? Rosie stared in disbelief at Billy King's back as he loped off in front of them on Bandit. She forced herself to focus on her own horse and tried to get him into the correct gait before the judge saw them, but all Scamper wanted to do was chase after the pony that had bumped him. He fought against the bit and continued to toss his head. They were halfway around the arena before Rosie could get him settled down and into a smooth lope.

Rosie fumed. She knew they had blown any chance of winning the class. *Why had Billy done that? It couldn't have been an accident.*

The announcer called for everyone to line up in the center of the arena. Rosie made sure she was as far from Billy as she could get. She stared down at her saddle horn. She was already fighting back tears and knew if she looked out at her family in the bleachers the flood would begin.

Although there was no way they would win the class now, Rosie hoped for at least a fifth or sixth place ribbon. The announcer began calling out the winners. After fourth place, Rosie slumped in the saddle. She knew they wouldn't win anything at all.

First place was announced last—Billy King.

How was that possible? Hadn't the judge seen Billy cut her off? Why would he give him first place?

Billy smiled broadly and tipped his cowboy hat toward the judge as he rode Bandit over to collect his trophy and ribbon.

Rosie's eyes burned, and the tears started to fall. She would have been okay with not winning; after all, it was Scamper's first show—but not to place at all? Suddenly she realized the other contestants were leaving the arena. Numbly she signaled Scamper to walk and followed them out the exit gate.

She spotted her family at the practice arena and turned Scamper in that direction, wiping the tears away with her shirt sleeve. She hated to cry, and it was even worse when others saw her crying.

Jared was the first to reach her. "You were the best! You would have won if it weren't for Billy's dirty trick."

"I hate him!" Rosie burst out.

"Now, Rosie—" Kristy began.

"I do, Mom. He's mean and nasty. I can't stand him. He hurt Bandit yesterday, and he ran into Scamper on purpose so we wouldn't win the class."

"We'll talk about that later." Eric reached up over Scamper's back and put his arm around Rosie's waist. He hugged her, then started walking away. "I believe I'll go have a few words with that boy."

Kristy's eyes grew wide. "Eric, promise me you won't do anything crazy!"

"No one messes with my daughter," Eric frowned. "Excuse me… pardon me…" He made his way through a group of people and was soon out of sight.

"Oh, my. I hope he doesn't hurt Billy." Kristy patted Rosie's leg. "You two looked great out there. That was very impressive for his first show."

Grandma agreed. "You were fantastic!" She helped Rosie down and gave her a hug. "Scamper deserves a treat. Why don't you and Carrie grab some carrots from the camper while we unsaddle him for you?"

Carrie walked quietly alongside Rosie for a few moments. "I'm sorry. I thought we would both win. It's not as much fun for me now, after what happened to you."

"I really wanted to win a trophy—or at least a ribbon." Rosie stared at the ground and scuffed her boot in the dust. "I had a spot picked out for it, right beside the last one my mom won."

"You can have my ribbon," Carrie offered, "and I'll keep the trophy. That way we'll both have something."

"Thanks, but no." Rosie shook her head. "You keep it. I need to earn my own."

"I know you'll win sometime. Scamper did really well, except for right at the end."

Rosie brightened. "Yeah. I guess he did."

By the time the girls returned to the horse tent with the carrots, Rosie felt better. Scamper and Kezzie snatched the carrots and crunched them loudly. "He's ready for some fair fries now."

"Oh no, you don't!" Kristy said. "It sounds like Grandma's been telling you stories again."

Rosie nodded.

"All right, everyone. I have to leave to get ready for tonight." Grandma gave the girls a hug. "I'll see both of you later at Carrie's house."

"What?" Carrie had a blank look on her face. "You're coming to my house?"

Rosie saw her mother glance at Grandma, and the two smiled. "What's going on? Do you guys have a secret or something?"

"You'll find out," Kristy replied mysteriously.

22
Carrie's Surprise

That evening, Kristy, Eric, Grandma, and the girls joined Carrie's foster parents for dinner. After the meal, they watched the video of the horse show.

"Carrie, you look so serious," Judy said. "I thought you loved to ride."

Carrie smiled. "I do. I was a little nervous." She had never seen video of herself riding. She actually didn't look too bad. Maybe someday she would be able to ride as well as Rosie.

Judy gave Carrie a hug when her class on the video ended. "I don't know much about horses, but you looked great. It's no wonder you won first place. I'm so proud of you."

Both Judy and Ross were upset when they watched the part of Rosie's class where Billy cut her off and bumped Scamper.

"Can't something be done about that?" Ross asked. "You have proof of it right here."

Grandma shook her head. "No. It's not worth making a fuss about. Rosie learned a valuable lesson today. It's fun to win horse shows, but it's not the end of the world when you lose."

Grandma patted Rosie's leg and smiled. "Life goes on, and your family still loves you."

"I know," Rosie said. "But I still wish I had won!"

"I've always told the girls," Grandma continued, "that what's more important than a trophy, is receiving the ultimate prize—when we stand before Christ and hear Him say, 'Well done, thou good and faithful servant.'"[1]

Judy smiled. "I'm always amazed at how you're able to tie everything back to your faith. Who would have thought there were so many spiritual lessons from horses."

Carrie looked around the room as everyone grew quiet. She saw Judy glance at Kristy, who gave a quick, nervous nod. Something seemed to be going on. Apparently, this evening had been planned, but she hadn't been told anything about it.

Judy patted the couch, inviting Carrie to come and sit beside her. She sat down slowly, growing a little worried. Was she in trouble? She tried to remember if there was something she had done wrong—or was it something she'd forgotten to do?

"Carrie," Judy started to speak, hesitated, then started again. "I don't think there's any way to ask this, other than to just come right out and say it. Would you like to live with Rosie and her family?"

Carrie stared at her. "What? I don't understand. You're my foster mom."

"Yes, but I've been sick so much lately. I haven't been able to be the kind of mother you deserve." Tears pooled in Judy's eyes. "You wouldn't be far away, and of course, you could come and visit as often as you wanted."

---

1   Matthew 25:23

"Eric and I would like to adopt you," Kristy explained. "I mean—if you want us to. You and Rosie would be sisters."

Carrie was silent for a moment, trying to take it all in. "Rosie would be my sister? My real sister? And you would be my mom?"

Kristy nodded. "And Eric would be your dad."

Rosie's wide eyes indicated that she hadn't known anything about this either.

Judy put her arm around Carrie. "It's all right with us. As much as we'd love for you to stay here, we want what's best for you."

Becoming part of Rosie's family was more than Carrie had ever hoped for, but she also loved her foster parents. She would miss them and didn't want to hurt their feelings. "Are you sure it's okay?"

Judy and Ross both nodded.

"Yes. I'd like to live with Rosie." That was as far as Carrie's thoughts could go—having Rosie as her sister. She couldn't imagine having her own mom and dad—without the "foster" part in front of it.

Rosie let out a whoop and nearly tackled Carrie. Kristy and Eric surrounded both girls and hugged them.

Judy and Ross extended their arms to Carrie. "We're so happy for you."

Carrie gave her foster parents a hug and kiss. "I'll never forget you two. You've been so kind to me."

"Carrie, we have one more surprise for you," Eric said.

Carrie clapped both hands onto the top of her head and dropped to the floor. She was beginning to feel a little faint. What else could there be?

"You girls know how Billy King mistreated Bandit yesterday. After what I saw him do in Rosie's class today, I knew it was time for that boy to learn a lesson. To make a long story short, he won't abuse that pony ever again!"

"Oh no, Dad!" Rosie gasped. "What did you do to Billy?"

A slow grin spread across Eric's face. "I didn't do anything to Billy, but I did buy his pony."

"What?" Rosie and Carrie both exclaimed.

"You bought Bandit?" Rosie said.

Eric nodded. "For you, Carrie."

"For me?" Carrie stared at Eric.

"I think it's some kind of a requirement that all the girls in this family grow up riding horses," Eric said.

Family? As much as Carrie loved the idea of having a horse, that word—*family*—sounded even better. She was going to have her own family and her own horse. It seemed like a dream.

"After the fair, you'll bring Bandit home to Sonrise Stable, where he can get used to *his* new family," Grandma said.

"This was Billy's last year in 4H, so maybe his riding days are over," Eric said. "At least he won't be able to hurt Bandit any more."

Grandma smiled, brushing tears from her eyes. "God has truly blessed this family. Life has its difficulties, but God has a way of working all things together for good."[2]

Carrie couldn't find the words to express all the feelings swirling around inside her. Her world had been turned

---

2   Romans 8:28

upside down in a matter of minutes. "You'll be my sister?" she repeated to Rosie. "And Bandit is mine?"

Rosie sat beside her without answering.

Carrie had never known a time when Rosie couldn't think of anything to say. The girls sat on the floor, grinning at each other.

"You know what this means, Rosie?" Carrie asked.

"No, what?"

"You'll never win the pony classes at the fair now, because Bandit and I will be in them!"

The adults laughed heartily at Carrie's challenge.

Rosie joined in the laughter. "Oh yeah? We'll see about that!"

Draw Scamper with Janet Griffin-Scott

Would you like to learn how to draw horses? I'm Janet Griffin-Scott, illustrator of the Sonrise Stable series. I love drawing horses of all kinds - ponies, foals, drafts, donkeys, or mules - it doesn't matter, I love them all! In fact, when I was in ninth grade, I nearly failed art class, because my teacher was frustrated with me for turning every assignment into a horse project!

Later, I received a Bachelor of Fine Arts degree, but it wasn't until I had worked for ten years as a freelance artist in Canada that I was able to pursue my first love - equine art. My work can be found in over 650 stores.

In this first lesson, we'll draw Rosie's pony, Scamper. Here is the original photo I worked from.

With a dark horse, the challenge for the artist is to provide muscle definition so that you don't end up with a flat, black blob. Decide what your focus will be, and eliminate any unnecessary background details.

If you know how to use graphics software and have a digital version of the photo, lightening the image will show more muscle definition in the dark areas.

The first step is to break your subject down into its basic shapes: circles, squares, triangles, and ovals. For instance, we see the kite shape in his head, lining up his eyes. His jowl and muzzle are ovals, as are the joints in his legs.

His hooves are triangles with the ends cut off. Even his tail and ears can be seen as stretched-out ovals. His barrel looks like a banana shape, but is actually a sagging oval with pointed ends.

Making sure the outline shape matches the photo of the horse is the hardest part, because all horses are put together in a slightly different way. Spend lots of time on this first step.

Next, outline the shapes while carefully studying the photo. Sketch in the paint markings on his shoulder, using the underlying circles as a guide. It's important to study the photo as you work in order to get a good likeness.

Then erase the underlying shapes. If some of the outline disappears in the erasing process, gently draw it back in. Do a rough sketch of the markings on his legs.

Begin adding details of his mane, halter, and eyes. Add a few strokes of long lines for his tail hair.

Add small strokes with a sharp pencil to suggest blades of grass. To make it look realistic, aim the strokes in the directions grass grows, from the bottom up. Begin to add rough shading on his barrel, neck, and along the lower part of his neck (the Brachiocephalicus muscle). This muscle is usually in shadow due to its large size and shape under the shiny hide.

Next add large areas of shading to darken him. There are several different ways you can do this—by using long thin parallel strokes or circular strokes, then smudging and blending the areas with a cotton swab, tissue, or dry paintbrush. Crosshatching, where the pencil strokes go in different directions to darken the color, may also be used. Adding realistic shading and blending is the second hardest part for beginning artists.

Create darker areas by making several passes of the pencil over the same area. His rump, stifle area, neck, and barrel all get extra strokes with more pressure on the pencil. When shading, use the pencil at a lower angle to the paper to get a softer, wider stroke. Hold the pencil more upright to create narrower lines and tighter detail.

In this next step I **gradually darken the whole drawing**, building up the darker areas with repeated strokes and blending. You can use a kneaded eraser with a point pulled up to remove areas that get too dark. Drawing is messier than painting, so my hand smudges areas, and I have to keep erasing outside the drawing to keep the surface clean. Fixatives can be sprayed on the finished drawing to set the graphite. Also, there are workable fixatives that fix layers of graphite in between darkening layers, but I do not like to use them.

Notice the **small dark strokes in Scamper's white markings**. Look at the original photo again, and you'll notice this halo effect where dark skin appears under the light-colored hair. Some horses have markings with a straight edge, and others have this transitional area. I have darkened his belly and tail again with additional alternating strokes and blending.

From the photo, you can see that the light was overhead, making his topline lighter, with a very light area on his back and rump. Early in the morning or later in the day, the shadows are longer and at different angles. When drawing, always ask yourself what direction the main light is coming from. That way you'll get the light and shadowy areas correct. This is critical to making the drawing look realistic.

Scamper is a black horse, but you can still use darker areas to suggest the curves and angles on his body. I mainly use kneaded erasers for creating highlight areas and to clean up smudges. Vinyl erasers, when they are new, have sharp edges that can be used in small areas.

Here I continued to **add graphite all over**, stopping in between layers to blend with my fingers, tissue, cotton swab, and paintbrush. This is a flexible process that goes differently for each drawing. I erase small areas to add highlights, allowing the white paper to show through.

As a last step, for my professional work, I scan the image and open it in the graphics program, Photoshop. Of course, you should make the drawing the best it can possibly be before using software to manipulate it.

In Photoshop, I: remove smudged areas, change uneven lead areas with the healing brush, use the burn and dodge tools to lighten or darken selective areas, and adjust the levels to darken the entire drawing so it more closely matches the photo. As a beginning artist, you should focus on improving your drawing skills. However if you want to experiment with graphics software, programs like GIMP or Paint.net offer many of the same tools for free.

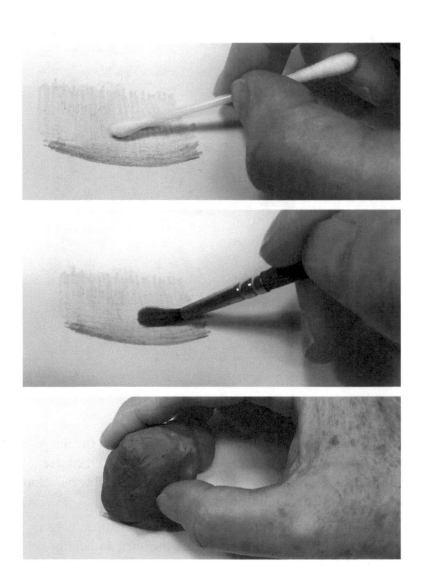

Blending Techniques

Cotton swabs have a soft, smooth surface that is wonderful for moving areas of graphite around and making the darker areas blend nicely into lighter ones.

Paintbrush – If the drawn lines show up too contrasty, they can be blended with a clean, dry paintbrush. Wash the paintbrush carefully after this to avoid damaging it or contaminating your paint.

Eraser – Normally the kneaded eraser is used to remove areas, but if a flat part of the eraser is gently rubbed on the surface, it can blend and blur the strokes.

Some artists **use their fingers**, but I only do that in larger drawings. In a small drawing, it's hard to control where the smudging goes when using your fingers.

Finally, you could use a **drawing stump.** This is is a tightly wound pencil-shaped instrument made of paper that can be applied to pencil media to blend areas. I have never liked them, however other artists swear by them. It's a matter of personal preference.

Crosshatching and circles -To get realistic blended areas, I make soft circles of graphite, or make alternating strokes going in different directions. If bits of lead come off the pencil tip and leave dark dots, they can be removed easily with a kneaded eraser. Remove larger blobs with the tip of an exacto knife. These are caused by irregularities in the pencil lead, especially with cheaper pencils.

Sand Paper – A fine grit sandpaper can be used to sand a flat area on the pencil lead in order to touch more of the paper. Most of the time you want to keep the pencil tip sharp, but for larger areas, this sandpaper trick works well. It also removes any grit in the graphite.

Pencil Pressure — By applying more weight or pressure with the pencil, it's possible to darken areas quite easily. You can tone them back with an eraser if they get too dark.

Highlights can be added by removing graphite with the kneaded eraser. The kneaded eraser is the most flexible of all erasers and can be formed into a larger shape to cover wide areas or into a point for more precise work. There are harder erasers and softer ones. Experiment until you find one that works well for you.

Feel free to **turn the drawing sideways** to make the shading easier.

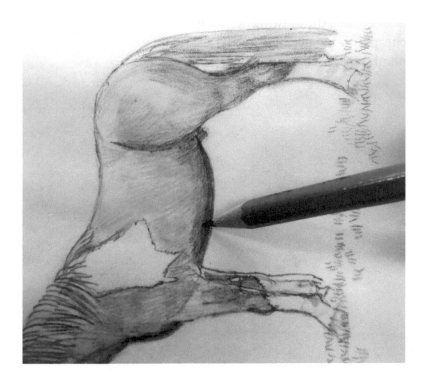

To develop an eye for horses, it's important to observe them in a variety of settings—at work, rest, and play. This is a good excuse for attending as many horse events as possible!

For most equestrian sports, the horses are moving too fast to draw from life. It's important to become a good photographer in order to capture the beauty of the horse in a still form that's easier to translate into a sketch or painting.

Photos from horse magazines or the internet are all right to practice with, but check for copyrights. If an image is protected by a copyright, it's illegal to use it for other purposes.

You don't need to spend a fortune for art supplies and equipment. Inexpensive cameras, or even a cell phone, will provide acceptable quality for your photographs.

I created the drawing of Scamper for this lesson with a cheap drawing pencil from an office supply store and plain bond paper used in photocopiers.

Don't be discouraged if your first drawing of Scamper doesn't look exactly like mine. I've been doing this for a long time, and many artists consider horses to be one of the more difficult animals to draw.

No one learns to ride a horse by taking just one lesson. Learning to ride requires continued effort and practice. The same is true for drawing. No one was born an artist. It takes lots of study and practice to learn to draw well. It's fun and encouraging to draw with a partner. Why don't you invite someone to draw Scamper with you?

Here's my guarantee—**you will improve**—if you continue to study and practice! Keep a notebook of your sketches, and you will begin to see progress. Draw Scamper several times and learn from your mistakes.

As Rosie's grandmother says, "Just do your best."

And whatever you do in word or deed, do all in the name of the Lord Jesus, giving thanks to God the Father through Him.
Colossians 3:17 NKJV

Join me for another art lesson in book 2—*Carrie and Bandit*. You'll be surprised when you find out who we're drawing next!

Janet Griffin Scott
janetgriffinscott.com

* Check the sonrisestable.com website for information on uploading your artwork for display on the site.

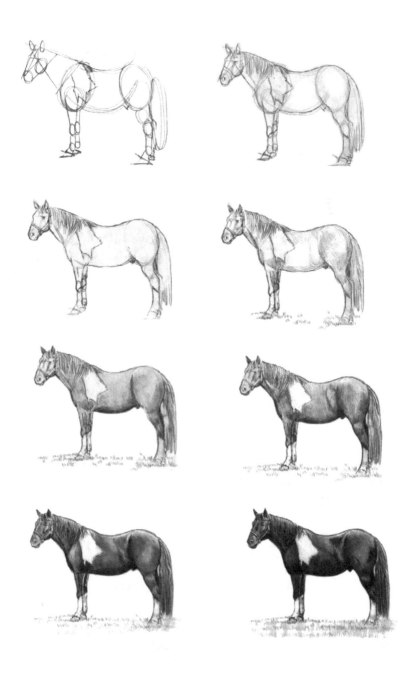

188

Horse Safety

Horses can be dangerous animals. You should take all reasonable precautions to prevent injury to yourself when you are around them.

The illustrations in the series may show riders without helmets; however, that is for artistic purposes. According to the American Medical Equestrian Association, head injuries account for approximately sixty percent of deaths in equestrian accidents. As Grandma says, "If you're on a horse, that helmet needs to be on your head!"

For a young or beginning rider, the safest horse is an older, well-trained one that has been used in a variety of settings: 4-H, horse shows, fairs, trail rides, and parades. Horses have different personalities and temperaments, just as people do. Look for a calm, gentle, well-trained horse when you begin riding.

The sequence of events in the book was sped up to keep the storyline moving, since training a horse is a long, slow process. Most trainers would not advise riding a horse at two. Many horses are still developing physically and mentally until they're four or five. It's better to wait until a horse is at least three to begin training under saddle. Even then, it should be several years before a young person rides that horse as they may be unpredictable until they've been seasoned with years of experience.

Young horses and young riders are usually a bad combination. As the saying goes, "Green and green often results in black and blue."

Discussion Questions

These optional questions may be discussed as a family or serve as writing prompts.

*Note to readers: The questions below reveal parts of the story, so you shouldn't read them until completing that section of the book.

Chapter 1

1. The Sonrise Stable sign at her grandmother's home was like an anchor for young Rosie, a source of comfort and stability. Do you have anything like that in your life? A landmark, building, or place that produces similar feelings for you?

2. Rosie's mother, Kristy, wanted her family to move back to the country. Do you prefer the country or the city? Why? What are the advantages and disadvantages of each?

3. After her parents, Rosie was closest to her grandmother. Describe an adult, whether a relative or friend, who has been a positive influence in your life. How could you thank them?

4. Rosie was amazed that Jet's winter coat was growing, to keep her warm over the cold winter months. Look around you (preferably outdoors). Imagine that you're seeing everything for the first time. What are some of the complexities surrounding us daily that we often take for granted?

(Book 3 in this series, *Clothed With Thunder*, goes into more detail about the incredible design of the horse and how it could not possibly have happened by random chance.)

Chapter 2

5. Fall was Grandma's favorite season. Describe your favorite season and what you like about it.

6. Were you as surprised as Rosie to learn that Jet was going to have a foal? Has your family ever raised a young animal? If so, describe what it was like and how you helped.

7. Rosie enjoyed helping her grandmother at Sonrise Stable. Horses require a lot of work every day—feeding, grooming, and cleaning up after them. Some young people love the idea of having a horse to ride, but are not prepared for all the work. If you don't have a horse, do you think you would be willing to put in the effort required to take care of one? If you do have one, what are some ways you can approach the work with a good attitude and make it enjoyable?

Chapter 3

8. Grandma read the Christmas story from Luke 2, to Rosie in the barn. Do you have any interesting or unusual Christmas traditions?

    (Book 8, *Operation Christmas Spirit* focuses on a special Christmas at Sonrise Stable)

9. Jet ruined the gift that Rosie had given her. If you have pets, you've probably experienced something similar. Describe a time when your pet has made a mess or destroyed something.

10. When Rosie heard an animal making a strange noise, she ran back to her Grandmother's side where she felt safe. Describe a time when something frightened you. What do you do when you are afraid?

Chapter 4

11. The horses were restless after being cooped up in the barn most of the winter. If you live in an area that has cold or rainy winters, describe how you feel as Spring approaches and you're looking forward to spending time outdoors.

12. There isn't any hurrying the birth of a foal. Rosie felt as if she "couldn't wait" for the foal to be born, nevertheless, she had to. If you've ever had to wait a long time for something, describe how you felt. Were you patient as you waited? Was it worth the wait in the long run?

13. In the Bible, God sometimes revealed things to people through dreams or visions. Can you think of some examples? Do you believe this still happens today? Grandma awoke with a feeling that something was wrong at the barn. Do you think feelings like this come from God? Should we always trust our feelings?

Chapter 5

14. Have you ever lost a dearly-loved pet? It can be quite painful, but unfortunately it's something many young people, as well as adults, experience. Do you think our pets will someday be in heaven with us? What does Scripture indicate about this?

15. You will sometimes hear people use the term "colt" when referring to any young horse, however the correct terminology for young horses is: foal for either gender, colt for a male foal, and filly for a female. Describe in detail what you imagine Jet's colt to look like—or draw a picture of him.

16. Grandma compared Jet's death to save her foal, to Jesus' death on the cross. When we've heard or read about the

crucifixion story often, we may not be impacted by the physical and spiritual pain Jesus suffered as we were the first time we learned about it. How do you feel knowing what Jesus went through to save you?

Chapter 6

17. Three months later, Rosie still felt sad at times about the loss of her pony. In Hebrews 2:10 it says that Jesus was made perfect (or complete) through suffering. God chooses to make *us* perfect through suffering as well. What do you think we learn through painful experiences that we may not be able to learn any other way?

18. What if Jet had been someone else's pony and Rosie had only seen her a few times. Would she have felt as sad? After the death of his wife, Christian author, C.S. Lewis said, "The pain I feel now is the happiness I had before. That's the deal." What did he mean, and how does that relate to Rosie and Jet?

19. The concept of a "pecking order" comes from the world of chickens, but it also applies to a herd of horses. The horse who is the leader (usually a mare) is dominant—the boss. The lead mare is not necessarily the largest or strongest horse in the herd, but she is wise and commands respect. The other horses submit to her authority because they feel safe under her leadership. How does the horses' pecking order compare to God's plan for us? Who does God ask you to follow, respect, or submit to?

20. Many people picture training a horse as dramatic and exciting—like an old cowboy riding a bucking bronco. However, when done correctly, training a horse is actually pretty boring. The trainer repeats the same lessons over and over until the horse's correct responses become automatic.

The trainer helps the horse form good habits. If you begin the training when a horse is young, when he is old enough to accept a saddle and rider, he usually will not object. How does this compare to Proverbs 22:6?

Chapter 7

21. Carrie persuaded Rosie to do something that Rosie knew was wrong. Why did Rosie listen to Carrie and disobey her grandmother? Can you think of a time when someone tried to get you to do the wrong thing? How did you respond? In addition to 1 Corinthians 15:33, what other verses address this issue?

22. Grandma tried to teach Rosie valuable lessons through the stories she told from her experiences as a child. Do you have any relatives or friends that tell stories like that? If so, what is one of your favorites, and what did you learn from it?

23. Why do you think Rosie would have rather had a spanking than not being allowed to be with the horses for two weeks?

Chapter 8

24. Why do you think Grandma told Carrie the story of Satin and Kezzie?

25. Carrie moved with her foster parents to the home next door to Grandma. As a result, she met Grandma and became friends with Rosie. Have you ever considered the people God has brought into your life and the purpose He has in doing so? Think about someone in your life, maybe your parents. Then think back about all the things that had to happen in their past to bring them together at the same

time and place. It's a great example of how God works all things together for good to those who love Him.

26. The chapter ends with Rosie indicating that she'll tell Jet's story to Carrie. As Grandma had said earlier, maybe the pony's story will help others understand what Jesus did for us. How do you think Carrie will respond?

Chapter 9

27. Carrie had been excited about riding a horse for the first time, but when it came time to actually do it, she was a little afraid. Have you had a similar experience when you were excited about something at first, but later were afraid?

28. Some people seem to think riding a horse is like riding a bicycle. You just push the pedals to go and apply the brakes to stop. If you can ride one bike, you can probably ride any, since they all function basically the same. However, horses are not machines. They have personalities. Learning to ride a horse involves learning to communicate effectively with that specific horse. What kinds of problems did Carrie experience on her first ride with Kezzie? If you've ridden before, what did you find the most difficult the first few times you rode?

29. Rather than wanting to have Kezzie and her grandmother all to herself, Rosie was willing to share them with Carrie. How do you think that will impact Rosie and Carrie in the future? Compare that to what might have happened if Rosie had refused to share with Carrie.

Chapter 10

30. Why do you think Rosie didn't just come right out and tell her grandmother that she was worried about riding

Scamper? Why did she make up the excuse that she couldn't find her helmet?

31. Grandma encouraged the girls to memorize 2 Timothy 1:7. If you don't already know it, you should memorize that verse also. Rather than having a spirit of fear, what should we have? What exactly do you think the verse means?

32. Can you think of people in the Bible who were afraid to do what God called them to do? Did they later obey?

Chapter 11

33. Grandma insisted that anytime the girls were on their horses, they had to have a helmet on their head. Do some research to see whether helmets are effective in preventing head injuries. Do you agree that helmets should be worn? Equestrian helmets are not the same as bike helmets. Do you think the current designs of helmets are effective in preventing injuries or would changes to the design be better?

34. The girls worked hard to bathe the horses and get them clean, but as soon as they let them out in the field, they rolled and got dirty again. How is that like 2 Peter 2:22? Warning: you might think it's a somewhat gross verse. Since every verse in the Bible is profitable for our instruction, what was God's purpose in including that one? What can we learn from it?

35. Sometimes even when we want to witness to people, it can be hard to find a way to get started. Grandma named her farm "Sonrise Stable" in order to make a statement about her faith and to create opportunities to steer conversations toward the topic of Christianity. What are some ways you could create Christian conversation starters?

Chapter 12

36. How do you think Carrie might have felt when the families arrived for Cousins Camp, since she was the only one who wasn't related to the others?

37. Rosie was surprised that her grandmother had included work projects as part of Cousins Camp. Do you enjoy working? Look up Colossians 3:23 to see what God has to say about our attitude toward work.

38. Jessie liked to trick people who couldn't tell her apart from her twin sister, Jamie. If you aren't a twin, would you like to be one? What would be the positive and negative aspects of being an identical twin?

Chapter 13

39. Rosie was determined to beat Jared in the egg and spoon contest. How do you feel about competition, winning, and losing? What is good and bad about competing with others?

40. Jessie thought it was funny to hit Carrie with a raw egg. What do you think about her action? Should the girls have told their parents what Jessie had done?

41. At a relatively young age, Jared was busy helping the men stack hay bales. Sometimes young people want to remain childish, rather than striving to become responsible. Look up Matthew 18:3 and 1 Corinthians 13:11. Briefly, one says to become like a child, while the other says to leave childish ways behind. Since the Bible never contradicts itself, what is meant by these two verses?

Chapter 14

42. The kids planned a campout in Grandma's barn. Have you ever been camping? If so, what are some of your favorite camping memories?

43. God created each of us with a different personality. What character from the book do you identify with most so far—Rosie, Carrie, Jessie, Jamie, Lauren, Jared? God can work through our strengths and our weaknesses as long as we submit ourselves to Him. Something like stubbornness is usually thought of as a negative trait, but it can actually become a positive (determination, perseverance) if we allow God to mold it for His use. What are some of your personality strengths and weaknesses, and how do you think God can use them for good?

44. Rosie let her imagination run away with her when she was frightened by the creature in the barn during the campout. Have you ever had a similar experience, where you were frightened, but it turned out to be not nearly as bad as you imagined?

Chapter 15

45. Rosie didn't like it when her father laughed at her for being afraid of the possum. How do you feel when people laugh at mistakes you've made?

46. Grandma didn't want Rosie to train Scamper for barrel racing at his age, because she'd seen horses ruined by contesting them too early. She wanted Rosie to wait until Scamper was well-trained and old enough to be calm and reliable. Contesting means participating in horse speed contests like barrel racing, pole bending, etc. Those types of events make some horses excitable, nervous, and difficult

to control. While barrel racing is not a bad thing, it was just not the right time for Scamper to learn it. Can you think of something your parents have said you can't do until you're older? It may be hard to see now, but trust that your parents have a good reason for asking you to wait.

47. What do you think about Carrie getting even with Jessie by splashing paint on her arm? Could there have been a better way to handle the anger she still felt about Jessie throwing the egg at her?

Chapter 16

48. Rosie's family and Carrie enjoyed their trail ride together. In today's world, people are often disconnected from each other even when they're physically together—because of TV, radio, phones, computers, etc. What's something your family or friends do that involves some good "old-fashioned" togetherness, fully engaged with each other with no distractions?

49. "The sound of swishing tails, jangly reins, squeaky leather saddles, and buzzing flies merged with hoof beats and the riders' voices to form a sort of trail song in Rosie's ears." This sentence attempts to create a word picture of what a trail ride on horseback is like, for readers who have never experienced one. Think of something you like to do, and write one sentence that describes it as completely as you can.

50. Rosie wished that she lived at a time before cars were invented so she could ride Scamper everywhere. What would be the advantages and disadvantages of traveling everywhere by horseback?

Chapter 17

51. In her story of being lost on the trail, Grandma wondered whether she might have encountered an angel (Hebrews 13:2). Have you, or anyone you know, ever had an experience that might have been an encounter with an angel?

52. While we are not to put too much emphasis on angels, and are definitely not to worship them, the Bible does indicate they have a role in our lives. Read these verses about angels to get a sense of their purpose. Psalms 91:11, Matthew 18:10, Psalms 34:7, Hebrews 1:14, Daniel 6:22, and 2 Kings 6:8-23.

53. Some horsemen claim that horses cannot think deeply enough to fake lameness; however Maggie's trick on the trail was a real experience, and it certainly seemed intentional. Do you know of any animal, yours or someone else's, that has exhibited behavior that seems to show them thinking through a situation at a level we don't usually give animals credit for?

Chapter 18

54. When you listen to Christian music, do you listen more to the tune or the words? Carrie, for the first time, began to consider the meaning of the words she was singing. What is your favorite Christian song, and what does it mean to you?

55. God uses different experiences in each person's life to draw them to Him. Through the stories from Grandma, Rosie's story about Jet, the loss of her parents at a young age, going to church with her foster parents, and the love and warmth she experienced from Rosie's family, Carrie came

to be saved. Describe how God has worked in your life or someone in your family. Everyone will have a unique story of their journey.

56. 2 Corinthians 5:17 states, "Therefore if any man be in Christ, he is a new creature: old things are passed away; behold, all things are become new." In what ways was Carrie different already? How do you think God will continue to change her?

Chapter 19

57. Rosie dreamed of winning a ribbon or trophy at a horse show. Was that a good or a bad goal?

58. When they arrived at the fair, Rosie was both excited and nervous at the same time. Why? Describe a time you experienced both those emotions at once.

59. Have you ever attended or exhibited at a fair? If so, what did you like best about it? If not, would you like to?

Chapter 20

60. Rosie enjoys drawing, and Carrie likes to write. Read Matthew 25:14-30. God gives each of us different talents and abilities that we are to use for His glory. What talents or special interests do you have, and how will you develop and use them for God?

61. Remember horses are not like bicycles. You could ride a bicycle in different settings, and it will always respond the same way. Horses need a chance to get used to different places or situations that make them nervous or frightened. Scamper was calm at the fairgrounds, until the carnival rides began with their movement and noise. How did he respond, and how did Rosie help him calm down?

62. Billy was cruel to his pony, Bandit. Read these verses, and describe how God wants us to treat the animals He created. Genesis 1:28-30, Exodus 23:4, Exodus 23:12, Deuteronomy 25:4, Job 12:7-10, Proverbs 12:10, Proverbs 27:23, Matthew 6:26, Matthew 10:29, Matthew 12:11.

Chapter 21

63. How do you feel about Billy's action that resulted in Rosie not winning a prize in the horse show? Why do you think Billy acted the way he did?

64. Rosie said that she hated Billy for what he did in her class and for how he treated Bandit. Rosie had certainly been taught that it was wrong to hate, but knowing how you're supposed to act, doesn't necessarily mean you will respond that way in a difficult situation. What could Rosie do to correct her inappropriate response?

65. Rosie's father was not pleased with Billy. What do you think Eric planned to do when he found him?

66. Carrie generously offered to give Rosie the ribbon she had won. Why didn't Rosie accept it? Would you have taken the ribbon? Why or why not?

Chapter 22

67. Grandma saw spiritual meanings in many of the things and events in her everyday life, especially related to horses. Jesus Himself, often taught by referring to everyday things surrounding Him: rocks, sheep, gates, etc. Can you think of an example of some thing or event in your own life that illustrated a spiritual concept?

68. There's something special about adoption. Kristy and Eric's choice to adopt Carrie is a reminder of how God chooses

us to be part of His family. According to John 15:16, "Ye have not chosen me, but I have chosen you..."

Ephesians 1:5 says, "Having predestinated us unto the adoption of children by Jesus Christ to himself, according to the good pleasure of his will..."

How does it make you feel that, as Christians, we are God's adopted children?

69. Do you think Rosie should have been told ahead of time about her parent's intention to adopt Carrie? Why or why not?

70. Grandma said, "Life has its difficulties, but God has a way of working all things together for good" Read Romans 8:28 to see the entire verse that forms the basis for her statement. How have you seen God work all things together for good in your own family?

71. What do you think life will be like for Rosie and Carrie once they become sisters?

The Sonrise Stable Series

Book 1: Rosie and Scamper

Book 2: Carrie and Bandit

Book 3: Clothed with Thunder

Book 4: Tender Mercies

Book 5: Outward Appearances

Book 6: Follow Our Leader

Book 7: Rejoice With Me

Book 8: Operation Christmas Spirit

Available at sonrisestable.com, amazon.com, and Ingram

Made in United States
Troutdale, OR
12/28/2023

16522599R00120